WATCHMEN OF THE HOUSE

WATCHMEN

Of the HOUSE

S.R. HOLMAN

RHWYMBOOKS
CAMBRIDGE, MASSACHUSETTS

to Chetan
and the workers in the slums by Sharan Clinic, New Delhi
with thanks

WATCHMEN OF THE HOUSE.

Copyright © 1997 *by S.R. Holman*

RhwymBooks
P.O. Box 1706
Cambridge, MA 02238-1706

Library of Congress Catalog Card Number 96-92295

ISBN 1-889298-59-X

This book is a work of fiction. Names, characters, places and incidents
are either the product of the author's imagination or are used
fictitiously. Any resemblance to actual events or locales or persons,
living or dead, is entirely coincidental.

Psalm 10 is quoted from the **New Revised Standard Version**
of the Bible (NY: Oxford University Press, 1989)

CONTENTS

૪

૪

"Remember your creator
in the day that
the watchmen of the house tremble..."

ECCLESIASTES

Death

❧

Arulai Samuels, who was 7 years old, knelt alone by the window behind the upholstered teakwood chair in her grandfather's library in the Delhi house. The space behind the heavy chair was dark, narrow and immensely comforting, like her grandfather. He was away, south, in Madras. She knelt by the window, looking south, but she could only see down through the mango trees to the locked gate by the street, where a servant was gesturing to an excited woman in a rich blue, red and gold sari. This woman was Arulai's mother and she was by this time very excited indeed.

She came soon after breakfast and politely rang the bell. Her appearance at the gate caused a great deal of heated discussion inside the house. When Grandmother refused to let her in, more heated discussion sent perspiring messengers hurriedly back and forth from the house. Arulai's mother, with all respect, would not go away until she was allowed in. Grandmother, with considerably less respect since she had less need for it, said she would die first. She told the servants to stop running about in the heat, pay no attention to the woman, and disconnected the doorbell. Left alone at the gate, and ignored, Arulai's mother began to call out to them in a loud voice, rattling and banging the gate, demanding to be let in, calling her children's names over and over again. This had now been going on for nearly an hour and it did not seem the least bit likely that she was going to stop soon, and quietly go away.

In the beginning Arulai watched expectantly, waiting for her grandmother to open the gate. Once she waved through the window at the woman, but in all the uproar no one saw her. When she saw the servants gesturing for her mother to go away, the child thought she might climb out the window and go out to the street by the back way to let the woman in secretly, but then found her grandfather kept all the library windows locked because of thieves. She dare not go into the hall since someone would see her and then she could not do anything at all. She knelt by the window behind the chair, listening to the voice that called out to her from the other side of the locked gate. She stared at the high, secured windows, until she finally began to cry; it was the only thing she could do. As she cried, the hurt grew until she did not want to look out the window any more. For two years now they had told her that her mother was dead.

She lay down and pressed her head against the soft, thick carpet, covering her ears to stop the echoing of her mother's voice. But instead of shutting it out she captured it between her soft, dusty fingers. The voice came in and took residence in the deep, warm channels of her inner ear, embracing the hollow places, intertwining itself forever within the sacred threadlike balancing wheel of the cochlea: her mother's voice, probing, provoking, releasing the sounds of memories she had forgotten.

The last time she saw her mother they were living with Uncle Willi and old uncle Harry on the other side of Delhi. It was the year her father died in the accident. Uncle Willi was rarely home and after Daddy died there was no one to protect them from the old man's drunken rages. Mama stayed in bed all day. At night Arulai slept with her mother and Peter slept in a cradle by the bed. The cradle came from Switzerland, her mother's country, where Arulai was born.

The last time she saw her mother it was the middle of the night. Her grandparents were at the house. She woke to see her grandfather wrestling with a drunken, noisy Uncle Harry. It was winter. Grandmother pulled Arulai abruptly from the bed she shared with her mother and she stood cold, shivering and very small, in a woolen shawl by the door. Her mother remained in the bed, unresponsive to the noise and lights, her thin golden braid hanging down to the dirty floor. Uncle Willi was not home.

Uncle Harry saw her staring at her mother. "Your mama's dead!" he said.

"She's not!" she replied. But no one heard her.

"Hush," Grandmother said. "The child's upset enough." But the old man leaned down and leered into the child's face. "She's dead, little girl," he grinned. His breath was sour and half his teeth were missing. The sheets in the new house were very cold that winter without her mother beside her.

But her mother was not dead. Even across the summer mango grove Arulai recognized her. There was no doubt. Why wouldn't Grandmother let her in? Arulai unstopped her ears to listen.

A door banged nearby. The girl crouched lower, wiping ancient dust across her wet face. Women's voices in the house chattered excitedly, chattered like the parrot they fed toast at breakfast, like two monkeys Arulai wanted to dance with in the park. At some point the voice at the gate ceased. But only the child heard it stop. She raised her head to look out the window again, just as the library door opened. Arulai curled up quickly in the darkest corner behind the chair as a greying woman in a blue and yellow sari hurried across the room to the telephone and dialed.

"Send the police," the woman said into the speaker. "We have a mad woman at the gate. What's that? No, I don't know who she is. It's very disruptive. We don't want this sort of thing in this neighborhood." She paused. "Wait - it's stopped." She paused again. "Yes, you needn't come after all. She's gone now."

She hung up and came to the window to look, her footsteps silent on the rug. She was practically on top of the child before she saw her.

"Arulai! What are you doing there? Get up!"

"Auntie Prema, why wouldn't Grandmother let my mother in?"

"You are a naughty girl, listening behind the chair. Come, come out from there. I'll wipe off your tears. Peter will be looking for you. You don't want to make him sad, do you? Come, it's almost lunch time."

Arulai remained on the rug. "Why didn't *you* let her in?" she asked. "You used to like her. Why did you call the police? I thought she was dead. And why did you lie on the telephone and say you didn't know her? I want to see her."

"Child, your mother's not fit to care for you. She only wants to hurt you. I thought you knew that. You should be glad she went away. She won't come back. Come. Stop crying."

"I want to be alone," Arulai said, looking away, speaking softly. "I promise I'll come out soon." Her grandmother would force her but Auntie Prema was more tolerant.

"You are an odd child," she said. "Very well. But come soon or I'll worry about you." The girl nodded and the woman went out and quietly shut the door.

"Liar!" Arulai said, kicking the back of the chair. "I don't believe anything you say anymore. I'll never believe you again! If Grandfather was here, *he* would have let her in!" And she began to cry again.

She fell asleep on the rug behind the chair, trying to remember her mother's face. Auntie Prema found her there long after lunch. She called the servants to come and carry the child to bed. Then she picked up the telephone again to call her cousin, Asha Mehta in Banaras, with the news.

🙖

Two months later, in late October, a nine-year-old runaway hurrying through an alley of India's most holy city called out to the other slum boys as he suddenly stared at gold embroidery on a woman's corpse in a mound against a shadowed wall. It was a corpse as big as a cow. The boy spent his nights prowling the ghats along the Ganges where they cremated the dead, feeling for jewelry and money. They called him the ash boy. Jasvinder, his boss, made him give over his finds at dawn every morning. Then he ate whatever the prostitutes would feed him, and found a place to sleep. But this morning his pockets were empty.

Slowly the boy saw the blood spattered everywhere around him. Long fingers of blood lined the soil, tinging the boy's feet, and scattered across the alley like handfuls of red rice at a wedding. In a moment six other boys came out of the shadows and stood around in a tight circle to stare. The fat shopkeeper who sold saris opened his bedroom window and looked down at the boys' circle, then hurriedly disappeared. His shutters banged and echoed in the dusty morning stillness. Other windows opened, more cautiously.

Women's dead bodies did not usually attract so much attention in this neighborhood in Banaras, but they rarely had this much blood to shed. Few were Western women and the boys had never seen a woman this fat, with short hair, wearing a Punjabi tunic with bluejeans and men's running shoes. The boys wondered if it was a woman or an obese man dressed like a woman. The corpse's eyes were open, and blue, and it gripped at its neck with bare, dirty, ringless hands, the Punjabi scarf wrapped tightly around the neck. The handle of a knife was barely visible under the body. The laces and bottoms of the running shoes were still practically white. The ash boy looked possessively at these wonderful shoes and the tip of a leather bag still wedged tightly under the corpse.

"Police!" someone whispered. The boys scattered quickly.

It took the police several hours to move the body to the morgue and process the belongings found in her leather bag. Identified as Jill Johnson, age 22, she had worked most recently as a freelance photographer for a portrait studio in New York City. Before arriving in India she had been living in France, in a guesthouse run by a group of nuns near the Swiss border. The police found in her pockets a large amount of money and a quantity of drugs. There were no obvious signs of sexual assault and the Indian police chose to remain discreet and ambiguous about whether recent sexual contact had occurred. To some this ambiguity spoke for itself. Indeed, before very long it became clear that the publicity of Jill's death was likely to cause acute

6

embarrassment to a small group of Western missionaries in Banaras. The police were amused.

The two Western men who stood in the morgue with the corpse did not particularly enjoy one another's company and did not share in the general amusement.   John Carter, a police investigator from the American Embassy, disliked dead American bodies on principle. Whenever they appeared they disrupted his comfortable Indian lifestyle. He had to find the family of the deceased, who usually wanted to appeal to the President of the United States to impose sanctions against India and felt that this was the job of the American Embassy. The paperwork and bureacracy involved in moving a dead body across international boundaries required countless numbers of petty officials, and death always unsettled his wife, who wished he would push harder for relocation to Sweden. The sight of Jill's body in the hot morgue, the sight of the gunshot and knife wound, and the duty of going through her bag and pockets raised his blood pressure until dots danced in front of his eyes and gave him a splitting headache. When Thad Hoskins asked him to put out his cigar in respect for the dead, Carter wanted to punch him.

Hoskins was born with dots in front of his eyes, thought Carter.   The two met now and then at quiet international functions, but Hoskins had no social skills as far as Carter could tell. This was especially apparent in the presence of the corpse. Tall and boney with very short, greasy hair and round eyeglasses, Hoskins stared at the damaged body with an intense and awkwardly curious confusion. There was something indecent about that stare, Carter thought. How often did missionaries get the opportunity to stare at obese women lying prone with blood all over them? Carter went over to the window and glared out through the dusty glass into the filtered shadows of the street. I don't want to go to Sweden, he thought. Too much like that bastard. Too cold.

Behind him Thad stood, unmoving, in the haze of putrid, dusty light. It was true that Thad was a missionary. He had lived in the Banaras slums in charitable poverty for so long that the recent laws against foreign missionaries were exempted in his case. Holiness was important to Thad, holiness as he defined it. And the coarse, sneering features of the deceased did not reflect holiness as Thad defined it. Who was this woman? The only thing Thad recognized about her was her shoes. He had a pair just like them. Yet the police said he must have known her. They found in her bag a letter to him, a letter of reference from Joseph Paul, at the mission's Geneva office. The letter said Jill would make him a useful volunteer in Banaras during the short months of her tourist visa. If this was so, then why did she acquire so much money and drugs before she came to see him?

Thad stared at the unknown face and forgot everything else until Carter grabbed his arm and suggested in a loud voice that they might want to continue the investigation. As he followed Carter into the police car all he could see was the strange face of the deceased. There was something wrong. Why would the mission send him this kind of person?

≈

Carter, Hoskins, and an Indian police officer arrived before breakfast at the last known Banaras address of the deceased. It was a respectable compound of apartments near the Sanscrit University, at the outer edge of the sacred city's Avimukta zone. When a servant let them through the gate into a green, quiet courtyard shared by three ancient apartment buildings, faces

appeared discreetly in all the doorways. All eyes studied the
three men who stood in the courtyard and talked quietly with
Mrs. Mehta, the landlady. When she sent a child to summon
three tenants in particular, many nodded knowingly to one
another and sat down to their morning tea to see what would
happen next.

❧

In a long rooftop room in one of these buildings, Katrien
Samuels woke abruptly at the sound of banging at the gate and
gurgling water at the sink. Across the room a woman in a cotton
sari was drying her face on a towel.

"Ritu? Is that you? What's all the noise?"

"Oh good - you're finally awake. It's the police. They
want to talk to us."

"It really is the police, darlings," a third woman called from
the balcony. "Mrs. Mehta is standing in person waiting for us by
her front door."

Katrien pulled herself up from the bed and began to search
for her contact lenses. The electricity was out and in the dark
she accidentally put her hands in a dirty rice pot.

"Hurry, hurry," Linnet called as Katrien rinsed her hands in
the small basin of water. They could not pump water when the
power was out, and the two women, up before her, had used the
whole bucket. She took a rag and began to search for her
glasses.

Why was Linnet home today, Katrien wondered. Her
friend, the man she called Jasvinder, had come for her yesterday.
When Linnet was with him she usually disappeared for days and
came back late at night, never in the morning. Ritu and Katrien

9

always welcomed the quiet and the extra space of the room without Linnet. Until Jill arrived. Where was Jill?

"Three policemen," Linnet called. "Young, but not very good looking."

"Hurry up," Ritu repeated.

Katrien sat on her mattress and slowly got dressed. The room was a large one with four beds, two old dressers, a drainpipe for water, an alcove for cooking and food storage, and very little light apart from the doorway leading out to the balcony and toilets. Jill's unopened suitcase sat boxed in shadows on a neatly made bed on a mattress in the far corner of the room. Katrien wiped her old glasses with a clean rag and gazed absently at Jill's things.

"Are you coming or not?" Linnet called.

Katrien swore under her breath and hurried out, putting on her thongs at the top of the rusting iron staircase. She gripped the railing tightly, blinking and squinting. Each turn in the steps brought her directly onto someone's porch. All the neighbors, old and young, men and women and little children greeted her politely and watched curiously after them. By the time Katrien at last reached the courtyard by the old pump, facing the shrine in the garden, all of Mrs. Mehta's tenants and neighbors were discreetly peering over their porch walls. Mrs. Mehta stood in the doorway.

"What is it, Auntie?" Katrien asked.

"The police about your friend, Jill," Mrs. Mehta said in a voice every onlooker made it a point to hear. "Now what have you girls done?"

Inside, the Indian policeman introduced Carter and Hoskins while the Mehtas' servant, Arnold, brought tea.

"Mr. Hoskins works with a small organization known as PUCHSA," Carter began, "Do any of you know this group?"

"'Poo-shah'?" Linnet enunciated. "Do you mean 'puja'? As in the Hindi word for 'worship'?"

"It's an acronym for that, actually," Thad said in an eager voice. "It stands for the 'Prayer Union of Christian South Asia.' We were started in - "

"Mr. Hoskins, perhaps we can put off the history lesson for another time," Carter interrupted. "I don't think it will shed much light on Jill Johnson's murder."

"But 'puchsa' is completely different from 'puja,'" said Linnet. "I do linguistics and the sounds have no bearing on each other. The letters distinguishing the soft 'ch' sound from the 'j' sound-"

"If you please," Carter cried, his face getting red. Everyone was obediently silent. But only for a moment.

"Jill's murder?" Ritu gasped. In her job as an announcer at a local radio station, Ritu always read the news as if it were distant and untouchable. She was very good at it. But when the distant and untouchable appeared in the same room, she found it hard to speak. The only thing she ever did with boldness was read the local news into a microphone.

"Her body turned up a few hours ago," said Carter. "She apparently came to India to work with Mr. Hoskins' organization. But no one seems to know much about her."

"We know even less than you, I'm afraid." said Linnet. "She did leave her suitcase upstairs. Perhaps you should take it with you. I'm sure it is still locked." She looked at Katrien.

"She made it a point to tell us it would always be locked and she would be able to tell if we even touched it," Katrien said.

"She was always saying things like that.   Are all your missionaries so rude, Mr. Hoskins?"

"Oh no!" he said.

"You first met Jill when?" Carter interrupted.

"She just appeared at the gate the other day," said Linnet, pushing her carefully painted toes out from under her simple silk sari. "I thought she must have known Mrs. Mehta."

The landlady pressed her lips into a thin, disapproving line and clasped her hands tightly against her teacup. "The girl was a complete stranger to us," she said in a loud voice to the Indian policeman. He nodded and turned to Katrien.

"You are not Indian," he said. "Why are you in Banaras?"

"I live here. My husband was from Delhi. Mrs. Mehta was his aunt."

"*Was?*"

"My husband is dead. I wanted to stay in India after he died. Mrs. Mehta made that possible for me by letting me stay here."

"Banaras is hardly a typical Swiss village."

"Is that a question, Mr. Carter?"

"You have to understand, miss," interrupted the policeman, "That every non-Indian who knew the deceased is important to these investigators."

"I would hardly say I knew the deceased," Katrien said.

"None of us did," said Linnet. "That's what we're telling you."

"She wasn't the sort of person one would want to know," said Ritu in a gentle and reasonable voice.

It was true, Katrien thought, but only Ritu could say it so innocently. From the moment that afternoon when they first found Jill sitting on their steps, she was always gazing at them with a large, emotionless smile that seemed to register every detail. She followed them into the room and began to talk almost nonstop in the nasal tones of a hungry mosquito. She wore a large burnished cross and the ugliest Punjabi tunics Katrien had ever seen. She was not entirely clean. And she did not pray like a good Hindu, with reverence and private discretion, but in her loud public voice in front of them all. Then, on the second night, she made it a point to show them a pornographic photo she (said she) found in her locked suitcase, and accused them of putting there. They told her she was crazy. But she just smiled.

"Do you teach Dutch and Urdu to the prostitutes?" she asked Linnet. Katrien thought it sounded more a password than a question. Linnet was a part-time philology instructor in the University's international language program. Linnet cursed Jill, threw a dictionary at her, and left the room. It was strange. Linnet was usually imperturbable.

"But your husband is also dead," Carter was saying to Katrien. She looked up, startled.

"People die," she replied. "It doesn't mean I know everyone who's murdered in India."

"Your husband was murdered?"

"That's what they said. It was in Delhi. Three years ago. You can check the files."

"I'm getting married and moving to Texas next year," Ritu said brightly. "My fiance is doing his PhD in Houston. In chemical engineering."

"Good for him," said Carter. Thad Hoskins smiled warmly.

❧

13

In the following weeks the police phoned occasionally with questions but they never seemed to find out anything. Sometimes Hoskins, came to the gate and began to try to talk to Katrien about religion. She could put up with the police, she thought, but she didn't have to tolerate this. One day when he pulled the black book from his pocket a few minutes after he found her in the courtyard, she told him exactly what she thought of him. But her words had no effect. After that she told Arnold not to let him in the gate. When she saw him in the street she turned down through the alleys. Occasionally Arnold brought her a pamphlet Thad left at the gate for her. She threw it in the fire.

After an unusually dry summer, the rains returned and continued, later than usual. The monkeys tucked themselves into holes in the rooftops, or broken corners of the lush gardens to eat bugs and other pests even as they became pests themselves. Rain poured down, insects flourished, the river rose, and the beggars huddled up, crowding against Banaras' holy walls and hovering over tentative, stinking dung fires.

One Friday morning early in December Katrien and Ritu went out to the American Embassy to complete papers for Ritu's visa. At the gate of the cinderblock embassy they shook off the umbrella and explained themselves to the guard. Dank and mouldy, the place offered them a dense, stuffy warmth out of the sporadic rain which still would not stop. Green light filtered in from a central courtyard garden. They could hear hush echoes of faint voices and footsteps through the corridors. As they turned a corner, they met John Carter at the bottom of a short flight of metal steps.

"Mr. Carter," said Katrien.

"Beg your pardon?" He stopped.

"We met some weeks ago - Have you found out anything more about Jill Johnson?"

He looked at her more closely. "Oh, Miss - "

"Samuels. Katrien."

"Yes! And this is - " They introduced themselves again and explained why they were there.

"Well, Miss Samuels," Carter shook Ritu's hand in a distracted way as he looked at Katrien. "It's a coincidence. I was about to contact you again. Do you have some time to talk? I'll show you the office you want. It's next door to mine. Come in when you're done. Perhaps Miss - Patel - can wait outside."

"Do you think they've finally found something new?" Ritu whispered when he was gone.

"It's been a long time."

"Go talk to him now. I can manage on my own."

"He can wait."

"You're putting it off."

"So?"

His office was full of plants. A little bird flew in and out of a high open window. The window was narrow and showed only the courtyard and other walls. As the secretary let her in the sound of a closing steel file cabinet made a scraping noise that echoed in the cement room in spite of the rugs and the crowded furniture. A man at a grey metal desk in a corner looked up, nodded politely, and went back to his paperwork.

"Here, come have a seat," Carter called from his desk. "Did they take care of your friend?"

"Yes. Thank you."

"There are just a few things I want to ask you. Don't mind Chuck -" he waved to his companion - "He has nowhere else to go; this isn't a formal interview."

"Have you found out any more about Jill's death?"

"I have some questions about your husband's." he said.

"But I thought I told you - and the police - about that."

"I am the police," he said, "I wasn't able to access your Swiss file, and only have what was in the American files."

"Is something wrong with my files?"

"Not at all. Mrs. Samuels, perhaps you can tell me why your husband was murdered."

She looked at him, startled. He was a large, bulky man with dry wisps of long curly hair which billowed in all directions around his head. It was the only amusing thing about him.

"They said he was shot and stabbed. It was senseless."

"Murder is not usually senseless. In fact, there are some similarities between the two cases. You never had any private theories about why someone killed your husband?"

"What do you mean there are similarities?"

He opened a drawer and pulled out a small box. Inside the box was an ancient, dirty handkerchief. He probed it open with the end of his pen. Inside was a thin-handled sharp kitchen knife. Beside the knife lay the bent, squared off scraps of shiny paper, tinged with color. Katrien realized, suddenly, what they were: photos which had their middles cut out. "These scraps were in Jill's bag," he said. "The police found similar scraps in your husband's pockets. And the knife - similar to this - was in both cases still in the body."

"Old family snapshots?"

"Why do you think these were family snapshots?"

"Well - that's what people keep in their pockets. Arul did. Why would somebody cut them up?"

"I can think of many reasons people would destroy photographs. The question is, why did they only partially destroy these? Have you ever seen this knife?"

"You say Arul was stabbed with one like this? It's an ordinary kitchen knife. Where did it come from?"

"Jill Johnson's luggage. One exactly like it was also embedded in her body."

"She showed us a knife when she arrived. We asked her if she didn't think people in India had knives."

"Who asked her that?"

"Linnet, I think. She irritated her. She irritated all of us."

"Tell me about your husband's death."

"I told you I don't know very much. I don't know why there would be a connection. He was - out with friends. It was a holiday. I was home. We were living with his brother and his uncle because we didn't have enough money to live on our own. He - they came and told me. I - his body was too terrible to look at. I - they never told me anything."

"How long were you married?"

"Six years - three when we moved to Delhi. We were there three years. He studied in Switzerland - that's where I met him - but then something happened to his scholarship money and he had to go back to India before he finished. He was writing his degree and working nights."

"After his death they told you nothing at all?"

"That's right. His family took care of everything. I never thought about - anything else Why do you think someone cut out only the middle of these photos?"

"Were you missing any photos after he died?"

"I don't pay attention to photos. I don't even take pictures. We had some done of the children - studio portraits. He had those in his wallet, along with some of his family. He was working the night before he died. He had a job as a security guard. But why would he have a knife with him? He came home for breakfast. We argued before he left the house, so I don't know all those things I'm supposed to know."

"What did you argue about?"

"What the hell does that have to do with it?"

Carter sighed. "As I said, there seem to be certain elements in common between the two incidents and I hoped you might be able to shed some light on them. If we can trace these links, it might help solve your husband's death as well. You had never heard of PUCHSA before you met Jill?"

"Jill never mentioned PUCHSA. Maybe somewhere I heard it before. There are so many religious groups. Why? Is it important?"

"It may be," he said. "You haven't said why you and your husband argued on the morning he died."

"I'm sorry I'm being so awkward," she said. "Arul's death was a long nightmare. I lost a great deal from it and gained nothing." Katrien stood up and walked away from him to the window. "We argued - " she said a moment later - "about a religious book he was reading. I didn't like it - that he was reading it. One of those silly fights you regret when - something happens. Nothing to do with knives or family photos or anything. He was a Christian convert in a high caste Hindu family, and I often thought he took his religious practices too far. That's all."

"Such as becoming an ascetic?" Carter asked, "Giving up sex?"

"No, nothing like that. Perhaps I can leave now if you are done with your questions?"

"You misunderstand me," he said. "Abstaining from sex - even for married people - is part of PUCHSA. It is precisely why Mr. Hoskins and his friends find Jill's murder so controversial. She died among prostitutes, after all. You're sure you never knew Jill before she came to Banaras?"

"Absolutely. I don't know people like that."

"Is there any chance she and your husband would have had friends in common?"

"How could they?"

"You say your husband was a Christian convert in a high caste Hindu family. That is unusual and suggests that he knew missionaries."

"He went to a high school run by Anglicans - what you call Episcopals. You think the missionaries murdered him?"

"I don't know what to think," he said. "You don't seem to like religious groups."

"You may notice in your files that my father belongs to a particularly outspoken and hypocritical branch of American preachers. My parents' divorce was very messy, very loud. God was always on the side of the preacher with his shiny new car. Fortunately the lawyers were not."

"Mrs. Samuels - " Carter said gently.

"Call me Katrien," she answered quietly, staring out the window.

"Katrien - Are your children Indian or Swiss?"

"Both. I mean, one was born there and one here. You do know everything, don't you?"

"I'm afraid I don't. Where are your children?"

"In Delhi. With Arul's parents. They - took them away from me after he died. I - they said I had a nervous breakdown. I didn't. I will, though, if I can't get them back."

"They are in Delhi. You want them back. And yet you are here, in Banaras?"

Katrien turned from the window and folded her arms across her chest as she looked down at him sweating in his squeaky vinyl chair.

"Yes, Mr. Carter," she said wearily. "And I am here in Banaras."

Ritu chattered about the wedding most of the way home, as Katrien pushed the umbrella quickly through the stinking streets and hardly listened. All around them the poor huddled under the arches of the city gates, in corners protected by plaster walls from the smoke and imminent rain. Old women dressed in white, ghosts behind smoke, were cooking fish in the marketplace over dung fires. Merchants cried out, their shadows dimly discernible from the copper and cheap pottery bowls as smoke and haze rose along the walls and was caught in the many corners above the wet street. The air here was especially bad. It was directly above Manikarnika Ghat, where a hundred corpses were carried daily in the dry season for cremation before being sent off into the holy river in an eternal attempt to escape the cycle of reincarnation. The women passed a pair of nuns bent over some cadaverous old man. He was still moving. Katrien looked away. Many spent their fortunes and lives to come here to die. Flies buzzed, heavy as charcoal smoke around the crowds who squeezed between the boney cows and peeling plaster columns to pass through the webbed streets. The only bright spot in the grey afternoon was a line of colored saris hanging from a merchant's cart, flags against the ancient white walls. Through the arches in the wall they could see the crowds on the great steps or ghats along the Ganges. Women were washing clothes, stretching them out along the edge of the river. Others gathered holy water from the rinse for medicine and ritual bathing. Shallow dugouts floated here and there, fishermen and holy men, their voices calling out in a dozen languages from this sea of ashes, flowers and dirt.

People came to these ghats by the Ganges to sing, to exercise, to meditate, to answer the calls of nature, and to die. Few came on purpose to be killed, though they might as well. There was a movement among the educated to clean up the river but for most people the idea was a sacrilege, and many children got diarrhea, dehydration and died from drinking the water.

Children were everywhere in the crowds, among the poor, the rich, the dead, the merchants, everywhere. Wet, dirty, loud and for the most part cheerful, the children called to them as they passed. Ritu chattered about the children who would help with her wedding. Katrien pushed the black umbrella ahead, silent.

"Where are your children?" Carter's question echoed with the heavy smoke. Did she ever really know? They took her children away one night in Delhi. Old uncle Harish agreed with Arul's mother that Katrien was incompetent. He let them in when they came. Willi was away, as usual, but when he came in he believed everything the old man said. Old Harish drugged Katrien when she objected. She didn't have the strength to resist him. No one believed her.

She had been trying to get them back since she came to Mrs. Mehta's. Last month Mr. Mehta helped her find a lawyer and she wrote a private letter to her father-in-law. Arul's mother had turned against her, but his father was not as bitter. But would he listen? And if he did, what could he do? It was true what she told Carter: she felt she would lose her mind if she lost her children.

Of course, she hadn't told Carter everything.

Life

ॐ

They came inside the gate at Mrs. Mehta's as the evening electricity went on. An old, unfamiliar bicycle leaned up against the inside wall by the front door.

"I wonder who's come," Ritu said, "Bicycling over in the rain."

They pushed off their wet shoes and left them in the dank, tiled hall. Someone in the sitting room was laughing. The servant came out carrying a tray of dirty cups. He nodded to the two women as he passed. The laughter stopped.

"Who's there?" Mrs. Mehta called out.

"Only us, Auntie. Such a wet day. Who's here?"

"Come and see."

Ritu peered into the small mirror in the dark hall and worked at her wet, loosening braids

"Is that my baby cousin, Ritu?" The man's voice boomed through the door and over the open space between the top of the wall and the ceiling.

"Willi?" Ritu pulled herself away from the mirror with a glance at Katrien, standing behind her in shadows. "Come on," Ritu nodded with her head.

"Williyer!" she said, leaving Katrien in the hall. Ritu's voice was gay and forced. "You look well. What are you doing in Banaras?"

"What I usually do." he said. "Watch the corpses burn. Get cheated in the markets. So your father has finally agreed to let you marry this rich Indian boy in America?"

"We have been very busy with the wedding arrangements," Mrs. Mehta said, "And all her plans to go to the States. Did you meet the right people at the embassy, Ritu?"

Ritu nodded as she took a teacup from the coffee table. Katrien watched from the doorway. Willi looked up.

"Hello, Willi," she said.

"Well hello, hello, as they say."

"Katrien was so helpful at the embassy," Ritu began, hurriedly. "And as we went in we met that American man who came here - when the woman died - he knew just what to do. And Katrien was great."

"Ritu sounds like an American already," said Willi.

Arnold brought in a tray of cake and more cups. The cups rattled as he squeezed past Katrien.

"Katrien dear, come in out of the doorway. Sit down. Have some tea."

"Yes," said Willi. "Katrien, you look better than the last time I saw you. You're finally putting on weight."

"Willi - "

"Don't remind you of those happy days at our house? I probably remind you of Arul just by sitting here. Come now. No - don't deny it. You're not a very good liar."

"Willi, do you have to be so offensive right away?"

Mrs. Mehta frowned at the window. "We need more cakes," she announced. "Arnold - where did you go?" Ritu began chattering nervously about her fiance, interrupted now and then by Mrs. Mehta. Outside the rain stopped.

Willi was Arul's older brother. He was a big man with gold-rimmed glasses and a silver watch. Always too sure of himself, Katrien thought, with a ready tongue, unlike Arul who had been the tall, thin one eager for praise and approval. It was odd. It was Arul who studied abroad, while Willi got an official post with some office in Delhi and, as far as she knew, never left India. Arul once told her that Willi was married very young in an arranged marriage which did not work. He never spoke of his wife, had no sign of her in the house, and never said anything about her. "Never ask him," Arul said; she never did. There was between her and Willi both a great distance and an uncomfortable familiarity. Arul's death and the months that followed had worsened things between she and Willi, rather than making them better. She could never remember whether she had left his house on her own after they took the children away, or whether she was told to get out.

She finished her tea and poured another cup. Mrs. Mehta got up, beckoning to Ritu.

"It's time for Ritu's fitting," Mrs. Mehta was saying. "She's getting lots of new clothes. But you know she is eating so many sweets he may need to take everything out again."

Ritu shook her head and rolled her eyes at Willi. "Yes, Auntie."

"The more you cost the more he gets, is it?"

"Come to the wedding, Willi, and see what I get," Ritu laughed. "Tell me if he's worth it."

"And quarrel with your father over your value? I dare not tempt myself. I think that scrawny rooster at the door is your tailor. Behave yourself, Ritu."

Ritu shut the door, making a face at Katrien.

"Now," he said when the door was shut, "Are you well?"

"You really came to see me?"

"Why not?" he asked, lifting his cup. "You remind me of my brother."

"You haven't changed," she said.

He shrugged his shoulders and smiled.

"I'm well, I suppose." She let the silence fall between them. It stretched with the fading sunlight across the bamboo chairs and the white walls.

"It's very good of you to help Ritu," he said.

"Oh, let's not start saying kind things to one another. It'll make me throw up."

"Stiff upper lip as ever," he said, "While the lower one trembles away. Very well. I come as a messenger from my father. He told me about your long and very interesting letter. He wanted me to talk to you."

From within the house they could hear soft voices and kettles banging. Outside the gutters were dripping. There was a lizard in the garden, high on the far wall, warming in the evening sun. Monkeys screamed somewhere nearby.

"What did he say?"

"He said you have one month."

"What does that mean?"

Willi shrugged his thick shoulders and smiled until she could see the gold filling on the outside of one of his molars. "My father is laconic, like you. I thought you would understand." He looked relaxed and cheery now, ready to laugh tolerantly.

"I don't. One month for what?"

"Alright. Very well." He leaned forward, still smiling. "I will make it simple and clear. He said that you may of course

26

get your children back, but you must go to Delhi and take them out of India yourself before the end of this month."

"But - that's three weeks! Before Ritu's wedding. Before - anything!"

He leaned back and stretched out his arms along the back of the couch. The silver watchband glittered from the smooth, dark hair at his wrist. "You don't want them?"

Katrien stared at him. "You still think that?"

"Do I?" A small insect wandered across the corner of the blue cotton rug. Katrien looked away and shook her head. It disappeared quickly at the sudden motion.

"I want them." She kept her voice low. "I thought you really knew that, after -" She stopped herself and put the teacup back on the coffee table. She settled in the chair, folding her hands together and looking down at them. "But Willi - how do I make plans from here? Everyone knows everything I do. Where will I get the money for the tickets? I don't know where Arulai's passport is. The baby - does he even have a birth certificate?"

"Your 'baby' is three years old. And my parents have taken care of those things. My father will pay for the three tickets - but you must tell no one. In fact, tell Mrs. Mehta you are going to Hyderabad, if you can think of a reason." He was leaning forward and speaking fast, in a low voice that could barely be heard across the coffee table between them. "If that seems too much of a lie for you, tell her you need to talk to the immigration officials in Delhi. When you get to Delhi, go to my father's office. Jit knows about it - no one else. He will have all the paperwork and a place for you to stay. Not with Vijay and Uma. You need not say anything about that. The money Vijay stole from you in August, by the way - no, don't speak -

Uma's grandmother got it from him one night when he was drunk. She gave it to me to repay the cost of your ticket from Delhi to Banaras - and this ticket back to Delhi -" he pulled it out of his pocket and passed it to her quickly, "So we are even, you and I. Do you understand? Try to look calm. Even my mother must not know when you arrive or she will send them away. I'm sorry you must do it all by yourself, but - it's more likely to succeed this way."

"Is it? And if I don't go, or can't? Then I won't see them again, either of them?"

"'Either'? You want one without the other?"

"Don't be stupid."

"I am not known for being stupid. Do you think my father says things he doesn't mean?"

"He always says what he means. Unlike his oldest son."

"I don't know what you mean."

"You never wanted me to have the children back," she said. "Why are you helping me now?"

He smiled. "I am simply an agent of my father's good will," he said. You would take them back to Switzerland?"

"I have to, don't I? There's nowhere else."

"Your father is in America. Could he help you?"

"Don't spit in my face."

"That's right. You don't speak to your father. What else is it that happens after the end of the month?"

"What do you mean?"

"Just now - you said the end of this month was 'before-anything'"

"Oh, a woman who died - they say it's murder. She roomed with us for a day or two. We are all supposed to stay in touch with the police. I was hoping to find out what happened."

"Katrien, are you going to have a baby?" He looked at her in her still wet, voluminous cotton sari.

"What?"

"A toast." He raised his empty brandy glass. "Now that, especially, should make you want to leave India quickly. My father might change his mind about you. And Swiss-born children are much more valuable, aren't they?"

His gold rims flashed and the glasses reflected the dying sunlight so she could not see him clearly. Behind his head the insect was crawling up the wall now. She turned to look at the fuzz of sunlight coming through the iron grate on the window.

"You really haven't changed, have you, Willi?" she said. "I never know if you're insulting me on purpose or trying to make me laugh without realizing how rude you are."

"Judge for yourself. Which am I, cruel or insensitive?"

Katrien shook her head at the silk wall painting of Siva in a garden of peacocks. "Why in hell should it matter?" she said. "And what will I tell Ritu and Linnet about leaving? Linnet catches me when I make up things. I'm not a good liar. You said it yourself. I don't know how she guesses; she lies so much herself."

"Just disappear. I will have a quiet word with Mrs. Mehta after you are gone."

"Do you know Linnet? She knows the old man - Harish - does she know him through you?"

"I said no one." He looked at his watch. "Who is this Linnet?"

"One of my flatmates."

"Here?"

"Yes. Of course."

"And what is this murder?"

She told him the story. "We wonder if she was really a missionary. She seemed very unbelievable. She was with that group Arul used to talk about - PUCHSA."

"Most missionaries are unbelievable," Willi sounded distracted. "But I am serious when I say tell no one. Especially if - "

"Don't be nasty."

"Nasty?" He smiled. "A little impolite, perhaps," he smiled. "But it is only natural that I would feel responsible for esteemed Indian widows in our family," he said, "Especially the daughter of a religious man."

"Stop it, Willi! You don't know what you are talking about. Get out if you can't stop torturing me!"

Footsteps hurried in the hall and Mrs. Mehta abruptly pushed open the door. Katrien looked up through a blur of sudden tears. Willi looked serious now. For the first time. He had taken off his glasses and was rubbing his eyes.

"What is wrong?" demanded the landlady.

"I upset her," Willi stood up and put his glasses on. "I seem to have said the wrong things - or perhaps the right things in a wrong way. The tailor has probably stuck a handful of pins into Ritu. Do you have any more to say Katrien?"

"Thank you for coming to visit me, Willi. You're nothing at all like your brother. Now go away."

"I am going."

"Wait." she said.

"Yes?" They were both standing up now with Mrs. Mehta in the doorway. The servant came in to take away the tea things. Katrien turned her back to him, to all of them, to look out into the garden for the monkey on the wall. Always a monkey. All the walls in her life had them. Just then she heard one screaming riotously by the little shrine.

"The job you mentioned in Hyderabad," she said smoothly, "I'll call them on Monday if that's not too soon."

"Not at all," he replied.

❧

Long ago and far away, on a farm at the edge of a tiny village near the sea, there lived a very little girl with long golden curls. She had lived in this place for as long as she could remember with an old couple whom she called Grandma and Grandpa, whom she loved very much. Now and then a beautiful woman came to see her whom she called Mama. Mama cried whenever she came and cried whenever she had to go away again. She always told the little girl to be good and not to let anybody else take her away from the farm where she would always be happy and loved. Grandpa and Grandma were not always happy when Mama came but the little girl, being such a very little girl, didn't know why. She knew only that she herself was very happy whenever Mama came and that she felt very loved on the farm and didn't want to go away.

One midsummer day when the little girl was five years old, she set out to walk through the farm and fields all by herself. She went out every day, sometimes alone and sometimes with her Grandpa. It was only a small farm and wherever she went she could see the house and her Grandma could look out of a window and see her far off somewhere. She liked walking through the farmyard and the fields by herself even if she was only five and the hay in the summer was almost as tall as she. She liked it better when she went walking with her grandpa because he would stop and explain things she didn't understand, but today he had work to do before lunch. So the little girl went off for her "adventure," which was what grandpa always called it. He called it that because, he said, you never knew what would happen while you were out.

She went first to the silver wooden shack by the orchard, just beyond the barn: the pighouse. Here it was cool and dark, full of grunts that sounded to the little girl like her grandpa after dinner. She put her feet up on the rough step and pulled herself up to look over the high boards at the old sow and all the little piglets. They were getting big and squealed with excitement whenever the little girl came in to see them.

From there she wandered through the orchard, down toward the row of pine trees that protected the fields from the sea far out across the fields, where the salt spray rose against the rocks and where the wind came from. The pine trees were as old as the apple trees and made a high wall protecting the orchard from the sea. It was a very old orchard and some of the trees looked to the little girl like old women, short and gnarled and rosy-cheeked with late apples. It was not a working orchard anymore. The little girl loved to run through the wild grasses and low scrub bushes around the trees, keeping watch for berries. It was still too early for blueberries, but raspberries would come in a week or two and blackberries after that. Between her grandfather's land and the next farm lay a long hedge of wild rose bushes with rosehips her grandmother made jelly from at the end of every summer. The rose bushes went right under the pines, all the way down to the sea.

Today the clouds looked like animal faces and the little girl kept looking up at them as she pushed her way through the grasses. She looked up once when she should have looked down, and tripped over a root, falling into the prickly straw and clover. It was warm and sweet and she thought at first she ought to cry but didn't. She lay there, face down against the grass for a long time, listening to the wind.

Ever since last winter, letters had been coming to the village post office to her from a man called 'Daddy.' The little girl didn't know 'Daddy' except by his picture which was in nearly every room of her grandparents' house. Someday Daddy would come and take her to live with him, the letters said. They said Daddy loved her. Daddy wanted her to be with him. Daddy's wife, Barbara, loved her too. When everything was ready, they would come. They were preparing a wonderful room just for her, full of dolls and pretty dresses.

Once she said, "But I don't want to live with Daddy and Barbara and have lots of dolls and pretty dresses. I want to live here forever and ever." But nobody heard her. Later she said it again but they looked at her as though she had been very, very bad.

She was still lying in the grass, rolled over on her back, looking down through the trees toward the sea, when she heard the sound of a car on the pebbled sandy road behind her. The white spotted cows in the next field looked up from their grazing. A black bird with red wings jumped up, startled, from the fat post where it was sucking out bugs. It flung itself into the wind, blood and black against the skies and, in a moment, was gone.

The car engine stopped. The little girl heard the doors slam shut. She heard her grandma's screen door slam shut. As curious as the cows, the little girl got up and followed the track back into the farmyard.

It was a big white car with silver all around the edges. Standing beside it was a big man in a white short-sleeved shirt looking at his watch.

"I was hoping to stay a few days but things came up and now I have to be in New York by tomorrow night and back in Baltimore by Wednesday night. You've had months to tell her and weeks to get her ready. My lawyers finally said to go ahead, and we can't wait any longer."

Then the little girl saw someone else in the car. A woman sat very straight and rigid in the front seat of the car. She was looking through the windshield, directly at the little girl.

That day Daddy and Barbara took the little girl away before lunch, and it hardly mattered that she screamed and cried until she could not scream and cry any more. It hardly mattered that she ran away screaming into the field again where her grandfather found her. He picked her up. She was limp, her face was all scratched, and she had wet her pants. Grandma quickly put her favorite, best dress on her and then Daddy and Barbara took her away in the big white and silver car. They took her away from the sea and the granny apple trees and the baby pigs who always squealed to see her when she went to visit them. Why did they let her go? Why? Why did everyone smile at her and wave as the car took her away?

Even in the car it didn't matter if she screamed or was silent, if she heard them or didn't hear them, if she beat her head and legs and arms against the seats or if she lay down silent, staring at the vinyl padding on the ceiling, which did not look anything like the clouds in the sky in her grandfather's world. Nothing mattered. The car went on and on and on, stopping only now and then to let Barbara and the little girl go to the bathroom. Whenever they did this, Barbara hit the little girl very hard for being bad. And the little girl always threw up. Once, on the New Jersey turnpike, she threw up all over Barbara. But even that didn't matter. Nothing mattered anymore. The little girl said to herself that nothing would matter ever again. And she was only five years old.

🍂

"Wake up, Katrien - You haven't told me what your inquisitor at the embassy asked you today." Linnet stared into the mirror with her mouth open, putting on eye make-up.

Katrien turned over abruptly in the dark, her heart pounding from the dream, from Linnet's voice crashing in. "He didn't know anything about the photo, did he?" Linnet had turned on only the small light by the mirror.

"No," Katrien opened her eyes. She lay in bed in the half dark. "He showed me the knife. They found one in her body when she died. - That's all he knew. Why?"

"Curiosity, darling. How do I look?"

"Like a whore as usual," she yawned. "Stop asking questions and let me sleep."

"You're in a vile mood. You of all people should be glad he didn't know about it."

"Linnet, go out to your wonderful men and let me sleep. What time is it?"

"Near midnight - no, after. You weren't sleeping very well, dear. And it's man. Singular. Not as in anthropos. God forbid it should ever be generic. But tonight most profoundly singular. Except I suppose, two eyes, two arms, two legs, two-"

"Don't be crude," Katrien sighed.

"Something upsetting you?"

"Just a bad dream." She rolled over and put her face in her pillow. "You woke me."

"Perhaps you would like to come? It's fun, you know - very therapeutic. He has some friends, I'm sure. It's all quite respectable. You know these upper caste families."

"I told you - remember? Never. Really. But thanks anyway."

"Never is a long time, but suit yourself. At least turn over and tell me I look beautiful."

"Do you?" She turned her face toward Linnet. "Say, Linnet, what happened to that photo?"

"Photo? Which photo?"

"The one she had in her suitcase."

"Lost, somewhere probably. Long lost by now. No need to worry. Do you like my new earrings?"

"Another pair your cleaning boy found in the remains of some corpse by the ghats?"

"You are having nightmares. Take something for it. Sure you don't want to come? Ritu won't need you early tomorrow."

"No. You still look like a whore. Go away. I'm tired. Have fun."

Linnet was at the mirror again, holding up a hand mirror to see the back of her hair. "Did I ever remember to tell you that you got a hole in my sari?" she said mildly, "And the silk petticoat too - the one you borrowed for Delhi."

"Delhi?" Katrien had her eyes closed. "What about Delhi?"

"In August - remember? When you went up to visit your darling in-laws of the past. Surely you would not forget such a family reunion?"

"A hole? Sorry, I never noticed it. What kind of hole?"

36

"Burnt - like a cigarette. Not a tear; a hole. You must have burnt yourself too, straight through. I mean, we both know the sari was filthy when you got back, but I have a good cleaning boy. The hole was more difficult. Why didn't you just tell me? It was so embarrassing when I noticed - made me feel - peculiar - wearing a sari with such a strange burn."

"The sari is six meters long. How could you tell it was only one hole?"

"Simple mathematics by the tape measure. Each hole was a bit under a meter apart - about the width of your hips. We measured it as I took it off. It reminded me of what my ex-husband did to me once when he caught me trying to seduce his baby brother. But of course that sari wasn't so expensive."

"You want money? Or another sari? Mrs. Mehta would know a tailor who could repair it. She knows everything. I am sorry. It was not a pleasant visit. Delhi, I mean. I might have got a cigarette burn and not noticed. I may have even done it to myself. It was that kind of a visit."

"No kiddos to bring back with you? That would upset you."

"Aren't you late for your party?"

"Touching a nerve? You're all nerves, Katrien. You ought to see someone about it."

"You know I'm bad with my own clothes. You are the one who wanted me to wear your sari. It was a very nice sari. I'm sorry about the burn. I didn't know you had an ex-husband."

"Long ago and far away, as you say. The most stubborn man in North India. Wouldn't dirty himself to touch me after he found me with his brother. Got his family to cut me off - most of them, anyway. He wouldn't give me a divorce - good Indians don't divorce, you know. I'm sure he enjoys adultery as much as I do."

"Did you have any children?"

Linnet laughed. "You weren't listening, darling," she said. "He wouldn't touch me after that, and we were only married a few weeks. Anyway, don't worry about the sari. You'll pay me back soon enough."

"What do you mean?" Katrien's head was still thick and the room seemed very dark all of a sudden. When Linnet didn't answer she sat up in bed. "Linnet, talk to me. I'm awake. What do you mean?"

Linnet was going through a jewelry box comparing necklaces. Katrien sighed. "Do tell me what you mean."

Linnet looked up and smiled, her eyes dark, piercing and cold, reflecting the black pearls in her hand.

"Tell me," Katrien said more softly. "I would like to know when it's going to happen. Even if I can't do anything about it. Even if he is only three years old."

"No games," said Linnet as if announcing a nonexistent item on a dinner menu. "Anything else we can understand from you, but no games. It's him or you. You knew that. You bought your own life. Even if you decide now that you would like to be a martyr, you can't buy him back. He's not yours anymore. Do you understand me? You haven't forgotten your blonde, Swiss friend and all his little tricks, have you? Don't be stupid now."

For a long time the only sound in the room was their breathing, together, loud in the dark silence. Then the pearls clattered in the box. Linnet pulled out a braided chain instead and hung it round her neck.

"Exactly what I keep telling myself," Katrien fell back onto the mattress and covered her head with the pillow. "Don't be stupid. Don't be stupid. If I say it often enough, do you think my bad dreams will go away?"

"Undoubtedly. Get old Samuels to teach you his meditation. Alpha waves, I think you call them. It cures nightmares."

"Now you're being stupid," said Katrien. "For alpha waves you have to be asleep - at least, able to dream. Unless you're having a nightmare I suppose. Reality is the worst of all nightmares, isn't it?"

Linnet smiled and went to open the door out into the humid tropical night.

"Then go back to sleep, darling," she whispered.

❧

Trains run through Banaras in five directions, one southeast across the Ganges just below Rajghat, one north along the road to Sarnath and three going west, one southwest into the heart of central and south India, toward Bombay, another west along a pilgrimage route, and a third northwest toward Delhi. The trains are among India's chief testimonies to democratic self-rule. Almost anyone can afford to ride them, though you get what you pay for. And while nothing in India is actually private in any Western sense, traveling by train mocks the concept altogether. Omnipresent city crowds are at least always changing. While all your relatives and neighbors at home may talk about you - and everyone else - you at least can shut a door when you need to use the toilet. But in India where money is not time but space, not land but walls, unless you have quite a bit of it for transport, you cannot get away from the bodies and curious whispers of all your compatriots until they - or you - decide to disembark.

For example now, thought Thad Hoskins as he opened his satchel in the fourth class car pulling into Banaras from Madras via Hyderabad, every time he tried to re-read Paul's letter every aspiring schoolboy scholar in the car pressed toward him to try and see if they could decipher the English words too. Finally he stopped trying to read it alone and gave up altogether, storing it in his bag while trying to remember all he could from its one reading on the bicycle rickshaw to the train station in Madras.

Mostly he sat and wondered why the agency was calling him out of India back to mission headquarters in Geneva. The cost of living in Switzerland was a hundred times what it was here. Wasn't he cheaper to support if he stayed? What good were his skills in coping with Indian bureacracy in Switzerland where schedules defined reality, where people actually stood in queues and waited their turn, where cashiers in the shops always had change if they owed it to you, and where no one was allowed, if the landlord put them out, to pitch a permanent tent on the sidewalk? What good would he be in such an ordered society? What could he do that any civilized Christian couldn't do better?

He hadn't come out to India because of any gift for the language, or even any sense of calling. He'd come - rather, well, this wasn't the time to think about that again. A rainy morning in an ugly chapel. That's all it was. Standing in a dress suit, waiting what seemed like hours, while all his mother's friends started to gossip that the bride wasn't coming. Anyhow, it was so long ago. Celibacy wasn't as bad as he had expected at first. The two weeks after the wedding date, when he drove through

England trying to find Gillian, that was the worst of it. She never did tell him why she changed her mind the morning of the wedding. Her mother had to tell him she wasn't coming. She never returned his ring. Not that he cared about the money, but he always wondered if she still wore it, if she thought of him at all anymore...

And now he had been stood up by another woman, a woman he didn't even know was coming, a woman who like Gillian was not what she appeared. All the paperwork for every prospective field staff went across Paul's desk. And Paul, his long-distance supervisor in Geneva, had known nothing at all about her. He never heard, he said, of one Jill Johnson from America. Nothing. Not one letter. Not even a similar name in the files. It wasn't such a large mission that she would come through anyone else, either. PUCHSA was really just a non-profit printing company that helped other missions print Bibles in forms that poor and rich might want to buy, and be able to afford. There were evangelism groups, of course. All night prayer meetings. You need that when you can barely afford air postage between England, Geneva and Madras. There was a strict policy against mass mailing fund raising. So if Paul didn't send her, where did she come from? And why? And where did the letters come from - ostensibly from Paul - on old PUCHSA/India letterhead? Paul was always saving money by using old stationary, and this had an address on it they hadn't used in years. But if Paul did not sent these particular letters, then who did? One was handwritten, and it had fooled even Thad, who knew his friend's hand over eleven long years of working together.

And then murder.

Was there any connection? Was it a nasty trick from someone who hated PUCHSA, but knew enough to have once been affiliated? This seemed more likely than the chances of someone from outside doing these things. Over the years, people came and went. Several had left the mission bitter, or with unanswered questions. Would any of these arrange for Jill to come and destroy its reputation? But - none who left were Americans. Most Americans like big missions; PUCHSA had very few American supporters. And who would add murder to it? A few had reasons to hold something against PUCHSA, that was true enough.

For example, the young Irishman, Timothy Green. Thad and Timothy had been at school together. Thad himself had converted Green and then persuaded him to come to work with PUCHSA. Even so, Thad never really understood why Green then chose to break all the rules they had, and even a few more, once he got to India. He had been in love, he said, but after all the girl was not a Christian, so that hardly counted, did it? And that certainly didn't explain his occasional drinking, or any of the other things that Paul had to throw him out for. There might still be others, silent with hidden grudges. You never knew about people. But, Thad thought, it still didn't make sense. And murder. That was an awful thing. Thad didn't understand that at all.

But maybe the people who murdered her were not connected with the people who sent her. Perhaps it was an accident, that the murder had happened to someone affiliated with PUCHSA. Yet anyone who could so cleverly imitate Paul's handwriting - and why would anyone want to? - would not be like the Christians he knew. He expected deception from other quarters. Not from people who knew Paul's very unique handwriting. And what was she doing out in a bad part of town so late at night? He couldn't figure that out. She couldn't have been a very good woman to be out so late. Who was with her? Whoever was with her would know. She couldn't have gone out alone. If he could find them, maybe he would find who it was who so hated PUCHSA to play tricks like this and why they would then raise a scandal like this in the organization. Paul was not happy. But why were they sending him to Geneva? It wasn't his fault.

Like an oxen, Thad threshed through the facts, over and over again as the train screeched into the city. It was hard to think and he kept thinking that he must do something - soon. In two weeks, if they got him the Swiss visa so quickly as that - and they said they could - he would be out of India.

Finally, as the train stopped and Thad was pressed flat by the crowds against the wall of the car, he thought of one more thing he ought to do before he left India. He ought to go back and talk again with the woman he had met with the beautiful, cold and tragic eyes, the woman who had so hardened her spiritual heart against him, the woman who knew Jill Johnson. Her eyes had followed him ever since the day Jill died. He would go back and try again to talk to Katrien.

⚘

Late that night in an old part of the city where the pink plaster buildings hugged together into a circle, and the young village girls in the upper rooms looked out onto an ancient dry fountain lit all around the narrow road by fires, lean and smoky, Harish Samuels pulled his fine wool shawl more tightly around his shoulders. He was Harish Samuels alias - well, what his previous names were he would not admit so much as in his thoughts, lest there was something to the rumor that some of these women had supernatural powers to read the mind. He examined the shapes of his kneecaps under the dhoti and pondered. India had affected him more profoundly than he expected. Over ten years ago, when he convinced that woman in Delhi that he was her long-lost older brother, all he thought about was safety. He had laughed about it. Who would ever trace him to India? What authority, knowing what he had once enjoyed, would expect to find him - voluntarily - on an Indian sidewalk? Time had a way of altering this original euphoria. Meditation had helped. To be honest, he wasn't sure which had more effectively dulled his acute awareness of discomfort, whether it was the meditation or simply lack of food. Certainly Linnet had helped.

He covered his wrinkled, scaling brown legs with the shawl and huddled against the wall. She was late tonight, he thought. The young village prostitutes would soon begin their most active hours and he felt unsafe here during those hours. He was old, after all.

As the old man pondered his kneecaps, a bent, old woman's shape, wrapped in a tattered shawl, head covered, came into the square, leaning on a young child. Slowly she hobbled toward the teashop where Samuels hid under the wall. The child, half naked, carried a bundle over his shoulder. He led the old lady solicitously along toward the gaudy bulbs lining the outer wall of the shop and the fires that would serve as light when the electricity went out, which it would do once or twice before dawn.

"Have you brought the tea?" A shrill voice cried.

"Yes, memsahib."

The shadow of a sari came down the steps in front of Samuels, down to the boy where he stood with his pack and dhoti, leaning on the wizened woman. The thin woman who came down to meet him had grey in her hair and pulled him by the arm, fiercely, up the steps and into the shop. The old woman began to scold her until a gentle hand passed some package into her arms, a package quickly hidden in the old shawl. Then the old woman abruptly turned her back on the boy and he was forcefully led up into the house where Samuels rested against the peeling wall.

"Psst!" He turned a moment later to the alley, where the same young, greying woman who had asked for the tea beckoned him. Sighing as usual, he got up, slowly, and found himself being clad in a ragged robe, with a child - a different child - pushed out to him in the darkness. Querulously complaining at such misfortune, he grasped the child's arm and let his new, young silent companion lead him out from the hiding place, out across the square, along the road to the outer gate. It was the same path the withered old woman would have traveled, had she ever left the small circle of hell she had entered for the sake of a tiny parcel. Old Samuels - Harish Samuels with all his aliases - went in and out of this courtyard night after night in his usual state of robust health. Perhaps he survived because he did not expect small packages.

Not far outside the gate he met Linnet and her companion, in the entry to another teashop, one where better-paying clients were sometimes permitted to take their companions. Linnet's companion was part-owner of this shop. Samuels never sought to know things about other people - after all, why cause them to lie if it was not strictly necessary? So, apart from the man's respectable economic status and although he had seen him almost daily in the two years since he had followed Katrien to Banaras, old Samuels still did not know the young man's name or anything about him.

Linnet put her arms around the child and wrapped it protectively in a warm cloak. It was only then the old man noticed it was a girl. Although he wondered that the children were always silent, his wise policies prevented him (sadly, he thought) from understanding this either. He liked to know about children.

"It is very late" he said to Linnet, looking wistfully over her shoulder at the silver pots and steaming bowls inside.

"She was late. Here, come home with us for a cup of chai, will you?"

This was Samuels' favorite part of these assignations. His shriveled stomach nearly growled.

"You know I do not take stimulants," he said politely.

"Yes, yes. Come along. We're all late now." The iron grip of the young man's arm behind the old one's back pressed him along.

They followed Linnet through the dark streets, protecting her from loose men and any who might wish evil on the child. As often happened, Linnet carried the child at the end. The child had begun, like a train engine just starting up, to cry. Linnet was unusually strong, the old man thought. He had always admired that about her.

No one bothered them, of course. No one would bother such a close-knit family on its way home in the respectable poverty of the Indian night.

❤

John Carter, the investigator at the American embassy, closed the files on his desk and pushed them away. He looked into his dirty teacup and found it empty, and put it down again. He sighed.

The Indian police were being very helpful in the case. Trouble was, they didn't seem to know anything. Anyone he wanted to see, they found for him. Any evidence he needed, they looked for, in vain. The only trace of evidence was the fact that this murder was like one in Delhi three years ago, the murder of Arul Samuels, the Indian husband of this half-American woman who briefly lived with Jill Johnson. Not that she knew her well. At least she said she didn't. But Arul Samuels had been more involved in PUCHSA than his wife admitted. Before his marriage and studies in Switzerland, he volunteered with the organization for a year. Maybe his wife never knew. Carter couldn't believe that a woman murdered in the middle of the night in a bad part of town was killed by another woman. He just couldn't. Who hated both victims? He had no idea. Other than Katrien Samuels, who was there who even knew both victims? He shook his head. He picked up his teacup again. Empty.

Motive? Not money. Not even to steal a passport. Jill's passport was wedged beneath her body. Besides, there was something strange about both deaths, something vindictively strange. Both bodies had been pierced through with the very knife found, wiped clean, on each of them. In each case, the stabbing was done after death. Why? Just a threat? Both Arul Samuels and Jill Johnson died because someone at close range blew their brains out. Only one thing was different about Jill's evidence: Police had found, in the bottom of her bag, a small, pocket-size photo album. An entirely empty photo album.

47

Slowly the wheels in his mind began to turn, like wheels on one of these village carts he had seen in the remote villages; he started to follow his thoughts. He picked up the teacup again and put it back into the saucer with a rattle. The phone rang.

"Yes?" his voice was as dry as the cup. He listened for a moment. "In Banaras?" he asked into the phone. The room full of high, heavy file cabinets and thick rugs muffled his voice. "Excellent. Put him through." He tapped his fingernail against the outside of the teacup now, then reached across to put his palm down on the file folders at the edge of the desk. After a moment he sat up straight.

"Willi Samuels?" he said into the receiver.

Angels and Demons

❧

Rain came at dusk while church bells were ringing up and down the lake. It was Geneva at holiday time in early spring. The tulips were out, white and yellow, shedding the rain which fell hard against the red #2 Metro bus opening its doors at the bottom of the rue Maunoir in Eaux-Vives. A short, stout, balding, surprisingly young man in a black suit carefully got off the bus and walked away as if the bells were not ringing, as if it were not raining, and with no idea that those involved with a murder in faraway India might soon influence his life very much indeed. His greatest present concern was that he had forgotten his umbrella.

He meant to bring it, of course. His mother, who lived on the ground floor below his flat called to him as he went out, saying it was going to rain. But, being the day of his ordination into the Anglican priesthood - something his Jewish mother did not consider very important - he had not heard her. Tomorrow he would go to the cleaners and see what they could do to make his new suit look as though it had not been rained on. But for tonight, what did it matter? After all, wasn't this section of town, where he'd lived all his life (except the last few years of school in England, when his ill and irascible father had demanded the son by his side) called Eaux-Vives, or living waters? So, what was a little rain?

He followed the steep stones of the street, climbing up from the lakeside, contemplating the rain in the splashing of lights. He hardly noticed the muted, still-clanging bells, hardly thought of his mother, or of the excited chattering on the upper deck of the red bus. He was thinking of the rain, and spiritual water. He was thinking, in fact, about the fourth century hermit, Jerome, who wrote to a young monk and told him that anyone who had been washed clean by baptism did not really need to ever again take a simple bath.

"Of course not," exclaimed the young Swiss priest to no one in particular as he turned left automatically onto the rue de Nante. "That is why I have forgotten my umbrella. Once baptized - dry for life. But when a man has just been ordained - perhaps I will never get in out of the rain again."

He sighed. He was quite used to talking to himself. He had done it ever since his father died and he had no one else to talk to. There was still his mother, of course. But with her, she did the talking for both of them.

"A life condemned to forgetting my umbrella," he mused as he came up to the house and started up the steps. He was really very happy. A light went on in the entryway over his head.

"Georges!" his mother called. Behind her voice he could hear the whispered hushing of the voices of the friends he had seen just that afternoon, in his glorious ritual of light, before the rain. He pulled the key out of his pocket and unlocked the door, stepping into the momentary darkness.

*

Several months later, on a hot July day, a young man wiped his brow as he came out of the darkroom into the bright fluorescent light of the photo shop on the rue de Lausanne. Business in Geneva was always brisk in the summer and the store

got its full ration of tourists buying film, or demanding rush work
and complaining at the prices. Timothy Green was faced with a
line of customers backed up to the door. Fortunately, the door
was less than three meters off. A German complaining about the
quality of his prints. A quiet teenage boy looking for an obscure
bulb size. Timothy had to check all the catalogs and then write
out the order to phone up later. Meanwhile more people came
in. An Italian woman buying film. A local businessman
ordering enlargements from slides and complaining about the
teenager holding everyone up. A student returning a camera case
he said was defective but in fact looked broken. Timothy sent
him over to talk to Stephen. An older woman leaving film...

The next customer placed more film on the counter. At least
film was easy. The "lunch crowd" would soon be disappearing
back to work, Timothy hoped. He looked up.

"God, what are you doing here?" It was his own voice. He
heard the responding slight shock of silence and wiped his brow
again.

"Sorry, it's just so bloody hot in here. Thad Hoskins, after
all this time. Back in Geneva, are you?"

They shook hands across the glass counter.

"Timothy Green?" said Thad.

"What's not starved or melted away of him, 'tis I. Something
wrong with the air conditioning today. They're working on it.
Important in here - you know, the humidity and all that. Bad for
film."

"You're back in photography, are you, then?"

"When the shop's not full. I'd love to chat old boy, but - "
he gestured to the line, which again reached to the door.

"Yes, of course. I just need this film developed. No rush. I'm not going anywhere. Can we get together for coffee or something?"

"Sure enough. Anything you say, old boy," Timothy held a pen over the envelope, "but tell me what you want for an address and phone on these? Last name still Hoskins?"

Thad recited his address and phone number. "How about after work today?" he asked.

Timothy didn't answer as he wrote. Then he looked up. For a moment Thad thought he was looking at a complete stranger.

"Love to," Timothy said suddenly with emphatic enthusiasm. "How about Gordio's - the cafe right across the street - around 7?"

The cafe was a tiny crowded place filled in the summer with locals and tourists. They sat outside and Timothy quickly sat facing the street. He ordered a German beer and Thad ordered Coke.

"How is their beer?" Thad asked, trying to be conciliatory.

Timothy laughed. "Have you given up teetotaling?" he asked, "Or do you still just talk about it now and then, along with hell and fornication?"

Thad lapsed into silence. Timothy was fidgety, he thought; reminded him of a caged animal, glancing around all the time, not sure what to do with his hands before the drinks came. His hair was long, falling into his face, and looked unwashed. Timothy and drink did not mix well, he remembered, and he would never forget once in India finding Timothy, drunk, passionately street preaching to a group of Muslim villagers who, fortunately for Timothy, found it amusing. Was he likely to repeat the incident here? No, Thad thought. More likely he would expect Thad to cover the bill. Even in India where they all got the same tiny stipend, Timothy could never cover his own expenses.

"Been a long time," Timothy volunteered. "Are you still a missionary?"

"Yes. But I'm here in Geneva now, at the main office. It's a lot of administrative work."

"Got tired of India? Ah, the beverages, they come. Thank you, love."

"Anything to eat?" the waitress asked cheerfully. The men ordered.

"No, they relocated me," Thad said, after she left. "Last December. It was very sudden. To tell you the truth, I wanted to stay in India." He talked for a while about people Timothy would have known.

"But good old Hoskins obeyed the Holy Spirit even when it told him to go to Switzerland," Timothy broke in. "Now, that's what I call sacrificial obedience. Damned good of you."

"Look, do you have to be so sarcastic? We don't have to talk about India. We can just have a drink as old friends, can't we?"

"Oh, darn, I'm being sarcastic. Sorry." Timothy shifted again, watching the street behind Thad. "When we were in school you at least had a pint now and then."

"I still do," Thad said. "But I have a meeting tonight at a chapel. I'm afraid the little old ladies will smell my breath."

"Be good for them. Most little old ladies have a nip now and then. They call it medicinal. Sometimes. My little old auntie was more honest - when she was sober, that is. Good old Auntie Kate. I haven't thought of her in years..."

"What are you doing these days?" Thad asked, patiently.

"Me? Apart from spending a great deal of time with the most down-to-earth French girl you ever met? I mean, she's almost Irish, the way she treats me like my mother, sometimes. Legs nothing like my mother's, thanks be to god. But you don't want to hear about her. That never was your cup of tea, talking about girls. You want to hear about my work, don't you? It's darkroom work, mostly. Still trying to show my photos. Sold a few here and there. Not usually at the counter like that. Girl was out today. Counter girl I mean. Not the French girl I'm not telling you about."

"I'd like to see some of your recent work."

"Yeah, well. There isn't much - not good, anyway."

"The street scenes you took in India were superb. Have you published any of them? I'd expect some of the international organizations here might be very interested."

"Yeah, well. They have their own photographers - and copy to go along with it. I've shown a bit. Here and there. Not much inspiration in the darkroom doing 'Lars' rush photos of little Inga feeding the ducks at the lake.'"

"Tourists are money, I suppose."

"Not much. Sometimes Stephen sends me special reproductions. You know, restoring old tintypes, making new photos look old, making fat ladies look thin. That sort of thing. But there aren't enough tintypes to pay my meager rent and most of the fat ladies spend their money on slimming fads, not trick photography, so - I stick with the shop. For now."

"Stephen?"

Timothy gestured to the street. "He owns the shop," he said, as if that explained everything. Then suddenly he pushed the glass and half-empty plate away. "Look, old chum, good to see you. I've - got to meet some friends myself tonight. Just

realized the time. Look - um, sorry to leave you like this. Here
- this should cover my bill. Keep following the Holy Spirit, eh
old man? See you."

He stood up and pushed the chair to one side. Thad stared
at him. Timothy grinned and shrugged and in a moment was
gone.

"Your friend left so quickly?" the waitress asked.

"I think he saw a woman," said Thad, darkly.

"Ah!" she laughed. "And you - you were not invited?"

Wearily, Thad paid the bill and caught his bus, reviewing in
his mind the sermon he would deliver to a small room of
missions-minded Baptist widows. At least Timothy paid for his
own food. That was an improvement.

🙢

Across the street the glass door of Strecker Translators, S.A.,
closed silently on the blue carpeted hallway. It would soon be
dusk; the city lights were all on. Katrien secured her satchel on
her shoulder and went out into the cool evening. Everyone was
complaining about this summer heat but she enjoyed it. In Delhi
it would be 110° by now.

She waited five minutes for the #2 bus and sat near the front,
watching the lights, preoccupied, content. She had just signed
her first book translation contract. Joanne's lawyers assured her
it would provide generously over the next three years, starting
with a hefty advance. Hefty by her own standards, anyway,
though Joanne had apologized for it. Finally she could repay the
Streckers the loan on her first month's rent. She could buy the
children good school clothes after all. She felt twenty pounds
lighter - all from the neck up, Arul would have said.

She got off the bus in the old city, at the bottom of the hill by the Lake. She bought oranges and some chocolate to celebrate - and a paper. She walked quickly up the steep, narrow streets, quickly out of habit. I could walk up the little Mole tonight, she thought, though the mountain had taken all afternoon and all her energy two weeks ago when she did it with Joanne, Jules and the children. She was always in a hurry to be home. Sometimes she would feel her heart racing as she walked home, and would need consciously to remember to breathe. As much as possible Joanne had given her work to do at home, but she often had to go out. Fortunately her landlady liked children and they liked her in return. Arulai could be trusted to a point but after all she was only eight. And besides -

She turned the corner quickly and shifted the groceries to get out her key. As she pushed open the door she heard footsteps on the brick behind her. She slammed the door hurriedly. There were always people on the street at this hour, she reminded herself.

Timothy watched the house for some time. He heard children's voices on the ground floor apartment, level with the entry door. The voices faded, and soon the lights went on in a room on the third, and then on the second floor. The street was quiet. Half an hour later he hurried down the cobblestone lanes, back to the lake, and into one of the public phones by the cafe. After he dialed he shook his hair out of his eyes and waited. When the connection went through he put his head down and saw, dimly, his baggy pantlegs and ancient Nikes.

"Stephen? Timothy. I have that address you wanted," he said quietly.

ەא

Sitting in the yard the following Saturday evening, Katrien was daydreaming about the Hauz-Khas ruins in Delhi. They stood, walled off from the adjacent village, abandoned and skeletal in a middle-class part of town. To get to them from the adjacent village, you had to walk down a path of broken pottery to the sentry wall and, from there, the ancient stone steps led up along the top of the ruin itself, or else down into the grass and brickwork above the three-story shell of square white pillars, stone porches and arched porticos. Here in 1350 Firuz-Shah Tughlaq built a *madrasa*, or college for Islamic theological training. He and several subsequent religious leaders were buried here, and at either end of the stone walls and pillars which remained of the college dormitories, octagonal and square *chhatris*, or tomb buildings, were erected over the graves. Although some of the walls had tumbled down, the roof and second story of the dormitories and lecture halls still stood and at dawn the sun came bright through the pillared rooms down to the flat central plaza which had once, centuries ago, been a lakefront. Now it was partly landscaped and rebuilt with flat stones and even a small stone bridge, taken up by the Indian government when there was talk of holding the Asia Games here, and then abandoned again, because the work could not be done in time. One could wander throughout the complex at will, through the open courtyards and long, ancient, empty hallways, and into the cool covered tomb buildings, lit on two sides by star-shaped sunlight coming in shadows through the stone grillwork above the doors. These small tomb buildings, half-walled gazebos, were a cool refuge from the incessant heat, a protective cell for beggars on a dark night, or a welcome place to run from a sudden rainstorm. Few tourists came here now, and the villagers for the most part left it alone. Occasionally in the night there were furtive shapes flitting among the dark stone - beggars, or errant boys, or bold couples not afraid of the spirits of the place. Looking out from the second floor stone porch that jutted over the complex, it was easy to imagine the ancient lake once reflecting the mosque and domes, the yellow stones and white square pillars. Students in those early days of Islam in India could dive off the porticos, or run down any of the many dozen steps for an afternoon swim, a break from their studies and the endless hot sun. Even now, they said the lake would fill in the rainy season, but in Katrien's daydream it was dry with the drought and the shadows of moonlight.

"Look Mama. Look at me!"

"No, look at me!"

"Peter, you can't do it as well as I can."

"Yes I can so! See? I can!"

The children were doing somersaults on the grass in the yard, occasionally managing to stand on their head for a brief moment before toppling over, giggling, onto the lawn.

"That's very good. Arulai, don't push him like that. If you hold up his feet, he can stay on his head for a moment."

"Hold up my feet, Mama!"

"No, me!"

Just then someone came out of the house and down into the yard beside her. It was Georges, the landlady's son. He lived in the apartment below, but Katrien rarely saw him. Today he was wearing a clerical collar with a short-sleeved shirt.

"Georges!" Peter cried. "Hold up my feet so I can stand on my head!"

"Do you mind?" Georges asked Katrien.

"No. Please do." She got up and went to help her daughter, who was struggling to coordinate a somersault so that it would result in her feet vertically ascending against the cherry tree. After several minutes of giggling, Peter decided he would rather climb the tree itself. Arulai ran around it several times and then ran to try the other tree in the yard. Katrien, letting them run, went back to her chair and her tea by the basket in the grass. Georges came and sat in one of the lawn chairs nearby.

"I hope your mother won't mind them climbing." she said.

"Not at all. I can't tell you how much my mother enjoys them," he answered. "I haven't seen her so happy in years."

"I hope the noise we make upstairs isn't too much for you," she said. "Sometimes they run through the house so, and I wonder that it doesn't shake your ceiling."

"Not at all," he said. "Children must be children," He looked at her kindly, squinting, as if he were nearsighted. He was short, just an inch or so taller than she, balding and pudgy, with a pink face, sandals and very pale and hairy feet. He reminded her a little bit of *The Hobbit*, the book she was reading to the children these days.

"Or the baby crying in the night," she said.

"Don't worry at all about it. My mother has had much noisier tenants. Before you came, we had four university students who played the radio constantly and seemed to take community baths at three o'clock in the morning. You and your children have restored my mother's confidence in the human race."

"You're a clergyman?"

"Oh, I've still got it on, don't I?" He unbuttoned the shirt at the neck and undid the collar. "I was at a conference all day. I don't usually wear it at home."

"I had no idea. Your mother is Jewish."

"She tolerates my belief. I tolerate her unbelief. We do alright. It was a mixed marriage - my father was an Anglican, I mean, though he didn't believe anything himself. You seem troubled by it."

"No, just surprised," Katrien said.

"And how old is the little one?" he asked, looking into the basket in the grass.

"Two months. I am sorry she cries so much at night. I had forgotten how hard it was when they're this little. In India there were always people around to help."

"You were living in India?"

"Yes, my husband was Indian. He - he died. I used to live near Vevey, years ago, so I came back here."

"I'm sorry," he said. "It must be hard to raise children alone."

"I don't mind it," she answered.

"Say, I know a fellow who just came back from India. He's an old schoolfriend of mine. Really, he's been back about six months now. Worked for an Indian mission organization in Banaras. Where were you in India?"

"I spent some time in Banaras," she said, carefully.

"You did? My goodness!"

"What is your friend's name?"

"Oh, you probably wouldn't know him. His name's Thad Hoskins. Worked for PUCHSA. But India is a very big place."

"Yes, I have met him," she said, wearily.

"Imagine that," he answered. But he looked at her kindly and didn't ask her any more about Thad.

"What was your conference about?" she asked.

"Oh," he put his hands around his knee and looked out at the children. They were both in the same tree now, telling one another stories. "It was a colloquium of clergy in the city talking about the problem of family and child abuse, and what we, as clergy, can and cannot do to try and help. It was very depressing. Very sad. I think that's why I came out when I heard your children just now. I hope you don't mind. We usually try to respect our tenant's privacy."

"It's your yard," she said. "How do you protect children from child abuse?"

"As clergy? Do you really want to know?"

"Why not?"

"Well, you have to start by being aware, of course. Often the abusive family will seem like the model family. People who abuse spouses often abuse children, too. You need to work together with agencies in the city. We had a panel of different representatives telling us stories that would raise the hairs on your head. You need to understand the complicated nature of an abusive relationship. Often the abused child or spouse will see the abuse as a family secret and remain loyal, denying everything. And, most important, of course, you must not assume you can fix it by yourself. There are quite a lot of referrals one can make. And if there is sexual abuse, of course, it is even more complicated and difficult. Especially for clergy like me, who occasionally hear confessions."

"Do abusers go to confession?" Katrien asked. "I mean - I understand you can't - I mean, speaking generally, you know."

"Yes, of course," he said, "Speaking generally. They may. Or a minor may confess that he or she is being sexually abused, thinking it is some sin of their own. I will tell you, I just recently became a priest, so most of what I am saying is generally speaking. But they might. And as a clergy person, committed to healing and wholeness of both body and soul, confessions like that could put me in a very awkward position, since I would want to report it to the authorities."

"And you ought to."

"But I can't. That is, I can't if the context is the confidentiality of confession. We're trying to work on how to deal with this. It's a more significant issue for the Catholics, I expect, where confession is something many people do. But if we learn of it in some other context it is much more straightforward. I may readily go to the authorities with details. And I can help the victim get out of the situation, if they will permit it."

"A clergy conference on family abuse," she said. There was an ironic tone to her voice.

"That - and other things. The things that happen to children in this city - well, it is worse in other cities. Amsterdam, for example. My parish is in the center of Geneva, so I may occasionally see children who have run away or occasionally those who might have been kidnaped. Though, they say, once they are taken they are usually not seen again." He mused, sadly, then looked over at her. "Say, I'm sorry! This is not a suitable conversation for you."

"It's alright," she said. "You couldn't make me worry any more than I do already. At least, now I will know who to talk to, if it should happen to my children."

"I don't imagine you as an abusive parent," he smiled.

"Thank you. That's not what I meant. One is always afraid one's children will - disappear."

"Yes?"

"Yes," she smiled back, as Peter came running up to them, his sister at his heels. "But you're right - it's not a good topic for conversation right now. Maybe another time."

"Mama, can we have ice cream?"

"Yes, Mama, may we?"

"Mama was talking with Georges. But it is time to go in, I think. Will you come up for some ice cream?" she asked him.

"Thank you, but no, I don't think so," he said.

"Peter, give that back to Georges," she said as she lifted the baby basket from the grass. "It's his collar."

"What's a collar?" asked Peter. Georges took the stiff white strip of cloth and showed him how it connected. "What's it for, a collar? A dog?"

"That's a story I'll tell you some other day," Georges said in a stage whisper. "I think your mother has some ice cream for you."

"Ice cream! Yes!"

❧

Late that night, when the house was quiet and all was dark, Katrien sat by the open living room window, the lace curtains breathing in the grey night air, remembering again the day last August when she went to Delhi to beg Arul's parents to give her back her children.

She had taken the only train she could get from Banaras the day before, and arrived at the carefully tended estate at the edge of New Delhi late the following morning. She had managed, somehow, in the filthy toilet area of the train station, to brush her hair, smooth and properly rearrange the expensive sari, and wash. She took a rickshaw to the house because the city buses would have undone in a moment the neat, cool effect that took so much of her fragile energy to create.

When she arrived, they shut the gate in her face. When she persisted, they threatened her with the police if she did not leave the property. She left in tears and wandered, blindly, through the neighborhood for hours, not knowing or caring where she was going. Finally, some time in the afternoon, she pulled herself together again and took a rickshaw to Uma and Vijay's house. They were once Arul's friends and when she wrote ahead they said she could stay with them when she came to Delhi. But when she arrived, Uma told her coldly that she was not welcome until after dinner. She walked out through the streets again, in a shabbier neighborhood this time, seeing nothing but the children playing around her, and eventually found herself in the only place respectable women were expected to wander, a nearby shopping plaza. There, still in Linnet's elegant borrowed sari, she saw nothing in the shops beyond children's toys and children's clothes.

When evening came she bought some food in a stall and ate it, covertly, in a rickshaw on the way back to Uma and Vijay's. Only beggars who had no homes ate alone in public: beggars and children. When she got back to Uma and Vijay's, she found a visitor waiting for her, waiting particularly for her, someone she had not expected. Uma and Vijay were not home, but Uma's old grandmother had let him in. He and Katrien went out to walk in the cool, unseeing night. They walked and talked for a long time and, when the sky was full of stars, they found themselves in moonlight at the edge of the Hauz-Khas ruins.

From her living room in Geneva, she stared out in the darkness across the red slate rooftops, remembering the dry warmth and cool breezes of India, remembering the clattering of the gate at her husband's house as it slammed in her face, remembering the echo of that gate against her soul, over and over again, throughout that long August day last summer and into the night. It was not until the night, as they wandered slowly along the pathways and pillars of Hauz-Khas, down through the open corridors and among the rounded, Islamic arches, that the cool, quiet austerity of the ancient plaster and stone began to soothe, to some extent, the shattering bitterness of the day's repeated rejection and refusal which still tore at her, threatening to pull her mind piece by piece from her body. The presence of her companion for those few hours was her only small measure of sanity. As she walked with him long into the night, and in its cool stillness began to return back from the edge of her madness, her mind and body gradually found themselves again, found themselves troubled and driven, starving, an empty void with nothing to hold onto. There among the shadows of the ancient yellow pillars this man's characteristically unshakable confidence, this man she had long thought she could never turn to, showed no arrogance toward her at all as he met her driven, desperate hunger with his own measure. Their lovemaking was an even exchange, but it was not without great kindness and, though she was surprised at herself, it calmed her. She remembered, afterwards, their soft, echoing footfalls as they walked through the stone porticoes. She remembered the moonlight in the shape of stars against the circular marble floor of the little Muslim tomb, the light of the moonstars and warm shadows moving along Linnet's borrowed sari, and the quiet hush and smell of a new-lit cigarette. Around them she could hear the distant sounds of one or two intruders out by the walls of the compound, but there was no one to threaten them, no one to bother them, no one at all who would drive her out from that place.

≈

Shortly after noon the next day, Georges was hanging his robes in the vestry closet in a dark stone church surrounded by Geneva's busiest streets. There was a knock at the door.

"Yes?"

"Georges? Thad."

"Come in! I'm almost ready." He still felt a certain awe for these robes he put on, and hung them up carefully, fearful that the women who came in each week to iron the vestments would think him irresponsible in his duties if his robes hung off balance in the closet.

"Interesting sermon," said Thad. "You're getting a bit radical in your old age."

"That's not what the bishop says."

"No?"

"No. Apparently I'm one of the stuffiest, most conservative Anglican priests in Geneva."

"Considering how few there are in Geneva, I wouldn't let that worry me. Where did you want to go for lunch?"

Soon they found themselves squeezed into a table at a nearby cafe.

"Say," said Georges, when they had nearly finished lunch. "My mother has a new tenant you might know from India. Moved in the beginning of June. Katrien Samuels. I was talking to her yesterday in the yard. She says your name is familiar - from Banaras."

"Katrien Samuels?" Thad looked puzzled, then stopped eating altogether. "Samuels? Are you joking?"

"No."

"I don't believe it. Blonde woman? Long braid? Sometimes wears glasses? Eyes - can't remember the color of her eyes. Age: twenty-six or twenty-seven?"

"What you remember is extraordinary, for you. Her hair is short, but otherwise you are correct. Three children. Little baby. Says her husband died in India."

"Children? She didn't have children in India - not with her, that is. Lived in one of those - what do you call it - hostels, with three other women. At least, it was like a hostel. Oh, yes, I remember. She did say her husband died. Murdered in Delhi three or four years ago now. The police thought it was connected somehow to a girl who came to work for me and was murdered." He told him the story, briefly. "I wanted to talk to Katrien again before I left Banaras, but they said she'd gone to Hyderabad. That was in early December. Little baby, you say?"

"Two months old."

"Adopted?"

"I don't think so."

"That is interesting," said Thad, looking puzzled. "You're sure her husband died three years ago?"

"I'm sure that's what she told the police - and me."

"Well," said Georges, looking thoughtful.

"I'd like to talk to her again," said Thad. "That is, if it wasn't intruding. What a coincidence."

"I don't believe in coincidences," said Georges, "But, to be honest, when I mentioned your name, she did not sound too excited about renewing your acquaintance. Forgive me for being blunt, old boy, but my mother likes her very much and I try to stay out of her tenants' lives."

"You sound a bit overprotective," Thad grumbled.

"Of my mother?"

"Well yes, that too."

"Look why don't you come have dinner this week. Say hello to my mother again. There's no reason you can't do that."

"I'd like that," said Thad. "You could invite Katrien."

"I don't think so. But you might see her if she's at my mother's house. Mama babysits for her now and then."

"And a two month old infant, you say?" Thad said, again.

"She seems like a very good mother," Georges answered. "Dessert?"

ɫ

In the early hours of Tuesday morning that week, Georges woke up in the night to the sound of a baby crying. It happened every night and it was true that he really did not mind. Better to have a baby wake you up than the incessant noise of voices that never let you sleep. He listened for a while, as he stared into the darkness of the night, expecting to fall asleep again, quickly.

Then, gradually, he became aware of another sound in the house. Out in the front hallway, through the open doors of the flat, he could hear creaking on the stairs. You needed a key to get into the stairway and there was a secretive sound about this. On his landing there were only two doors, Georges' and another, locked door which led up to Katrien's apartment. There was another door to her apartment at the top of the stairs, so she usually left this lower door open during the day, and locked it at night. Neither of the two doors on the landing were marked, since the mailboxes were in the entryway downstairs.

Slowly he got out of bed and walked quietly through the dark flat in his bare feet. The baby was still crying, above him, and it muffled the sound out on the steps. As he approached the

68

hall door he heard the soft, scraping sound of paper sliding under his front door. By the time he reached it, he heard the door to the street clicking shut on the floor below. He turned the hall light on and ran down in his pajamas. The entry door to the stairwell had been left open. No one was there. He ran into the street, but saw nothing.

Afraid to disturb his mother, he shut off the hall light and, shutting the doors quietly, went back up to his flat. He picked up the envelope that had been slipped under his door. It was a plain manila envelope, unmarked and unsealed. He undid the clasp.

Inside was a piece of plain white paper with a short message printed on it: "There are many more of these," it said. "Resist and we will sell them - and mail them to certain interested parties." There was no signature. Georges turned the sheet over. On the back there was a color xerox of a photograph of a young boy. He was about three, posing provocatively, nude. It was Peter, Katrien's little son.

"Mon dieu!" said Georges.

Just then there was a knock at the door. Katrien stood in her bathrobe on the landing, holding the baby.

"Is your mother alright?" she asked. "I heard you running down the stairs."

"I'm sure she's well," he said. "Someone just left me something I believe was meant for you."

Katrien looked down at the envelope in his hand. The photo was partly visible in the dim light from his entryway.

"So, it's finally happening," she said softly.

"I beg your pardon?"

She looked up at him, blankly.

"Nothing," she said. "I didn't say anything."

ѣ

Joanne Strecker often got up at 5 to spend an hour or two proofreading translations before her husband was up. It was a quiet time when she could think clearly, and concentrate without the phone ringing. But this morning it rang just as she sat down at the desk. Fresh air came cool through the window and with it the scent of morning blossoms from the garden. She looked at the clock: 5:14. Must be an international business call. But when the voice came on, she picked it up quickly. She listened to the voice for a long time.

"Are you certain about all this?" she asked. Jules, coming down the hall ten minutes later, glanced in at her.

"Coffee?" he whispered. She nodded. He disappeared down the marble tiled hall to the kitchen.

"I'll be right over," she said into the phone.

Present and Future

ﻪ

When Barbara first showed the little girl her new bedroom in a small town an hour outside of Baltimore, there were six dolls sitting on the white, quilted bedspread, waiting to meet her. There was a baby doll, a school doll, a bride doll and three Barbie dolls. They stared at her with their glassy, cold, plastic eyes while Barbara opened the windows and the smell of pine trees came into the little room. Then Barbara showed her all the new clothes in the closet and made her put on some of them. The little girl was growing tall that summer and some were already too small. This made Barbara angry at the little girl. I want Mama and Grandma, the little girl thought. But she didn't say anything. She didn't say anything, in fact, all of the first week and most of the second. In the second week some children came over to play in Daddy and Barbara's yard and the little girl forgot, for a moment, not to talk. Soon after this she started school and her teachers didn't watch her as closely as Barbara did, so she talked a little more. Soon she was talking more at home, but Barbara watched her closely just the same. Every Sunday morning, for one reason or another, Daddy spanked her, and Barbara washed her up, and then they went to church in the big white car. Barbara always put a lacy dress on the little girl and a headband that hurt her inside her head. She and Barbara always sat in the front row of the school theater where Daddy's church met before it bought a building of its own. The seats were a scratchy dark purple, and once the little girl found old

71

bubble gum stuck under the arm of her chair. She spent most of the sermon picking it off. When she put it in her mouth Barbara, who had been watching her for just that moment, pinched her and she screamed. They had to take her out in front of everyone. Daddy beat her hard for the first time that afternoon. She lay in bed silently that night, feeling the breeze from the air under the pine trees outside her window, and watched her dolls. Barbara had moved her dolls to the top of the dresser and they stared back at her, like Barbara, with their cold plastic gaze. Only the baby doll had eyes that shut. She liked the baby doll best, so Barbara often took it away from her because she was bad.

When the little girl was nine years old, she saw Mama again for the first time. They met in a restaurant, just the two of them, and an older lady the little girl didn't know. The older lady spent the visit writing things down on a piece of paper in a scrawl the little girl could not read. Mama told her that Barbara and Daddy were not truly married to each other. They said they were because Daddy's brother performed a ceremony for them in a church, but Daddy never gave Mama a divorce. The little girl found this all very complicated. Then Barbara and Daddy found out what Mama had told her. Soon after this they moved away from the house by the pine trees and the little girl missed a year of school, as Daddy and Barbara took a sabbatical, driving southwest into the mountains, preaching in a different church every Sunday and Wednesday night. The little girl didn't get any new clothes this year, and her baby doll was very ragged by now, so one of its eyes didn't shut all the way anymore.

Then, one Wednesday night in August when the little girl was ten years old, Daddy was preaching in a small wooden frame building at the edge of a parking lot in eastern Kentucky. The parking lot was full of old red and blue trucks, rusting into brown, with the windows all rolled down. Behind the parking lot was an old factory with many broken windows and, nearby, a diner blinked "Frosty" in neon lights that quivered and vibrated in the hot summer night. The little girl sat on the back steps of the church, sharing a red popsicle with two other ten year old girls, when a small, shiny blue car drove into the parking lot and stopped right in front of them. A very blonde man in dark glasses rolled down the window and looked up. Then the front passenger door opened and Mama got out. She wore a dark blue, sleeveless dress and low, white heels and she was very slim and pretty, not like Barbara at all. She came over to the steps, where red popsicle juice was dripping all over the three girls' knees and onto their plastic flipflops. She told the little girl that she had come to take the little girl home, after all this time. Mama was crying. When they offered her some of the popsicle she tasted it delicately with her tongue, smiled, and then cried some more.

That evening the little girl climbed into the car with Mama and the blonde man with dark glasses. They drove out of the parking lot just as the off-key piano in the church stopped playing and people began to run out the back door, stamping sticky red popsicle juice all along the old wooden boards of the steps and into the cracked tar pavement. The car with the little girl drove away quickly. The car with Daddy and Barbara also drove along the same road that night, more slowly, far behind them. The little girl fell asleep on the soft back seat, soft like a little boy's teddy bear she once was allowed to play with until Barbara took it away and gave it back to the little boy. She hugged the seat tight and listened as the radio played banjo music far into the night. She woke up once on the Daniel Webster Highway when, a little out of Louisville, a policeman stopped them and gave them a speeding ticket. But after that he let them

73

go, and she fell asleep again until Mama carried her up a narrow set of metal steps as the sun rose in the dense heat. Mama gave her a whole piece of bubble gum all for herself and the little girl stared for a long time at the cartoon inside the gum wrapper, before she fell asleep again. When she woke up the plane was ascending over the sweltering Kentucky farmlands, heading east, and the little girl was leaning against the blonde man in dark glasses, listening to the sounds he was making to her and Mama, sounds she did not understand. But they were beautiful sounds, more beautiful than the off-key piano, and she listened to them for a long time as she leaned against him and watched her mother fall asleep.

*

Linnet's Air India flight landed in Geneva midmorning the first Saturday in August. She made a few phone calls and soon made her way by cab to a very clean flat off the avenue Guiseppe near the United Nations, facing east toward the lake. She needed a vacation, after all. She told old Harish that she and Jasvinder were going up to an ashram in the mountains. It was partly true; at least that's where Jasvinder went. He wanted her to come, too, not fly to Switzerland. He was jealous of Stephen. Linnet smiled to herself. Jasvinder wanted to send Harish with her, but then the old man, as usual, disappeared. She could have brought him along as a relative, with proof she could support him for a few months, but his quiet little habits tended to be expensive to support. Better without him.

Somewhere in Geneva, she thought as the taxi hurried her through the broad avenues of the new city, someone knows about that woman who called herself Jill Johnson. Who sent her and why? Where did she get photos Linnet had been sure were destroyed years ago? Who connected them, in Banaras, with Stephen's work? It was in the best interest of all of them to trace this quickly. Nothing could interfere with her real reason for coming.

The maid let her in. Stephen wasn't home. She unpacked, and then picked up the phone. Changing her mind, she hung up again and went out. There was a travel bureau on the next street. Linnet made her arrangements, paid for them, and then went out shopping. By the time she got back to the flat Stephen was back, and it was dinnertime.

Down on the street, leaning against a black steel chair at a table outside the cafe, another man lit a cigarette and watched the flat for an hour after Linnet returned. He felt out of place in his white shirt, white pants and Indian sandals, but that could not be helped. He had followed Linnet from the airport and had not yet had time to change. At least she had not seen him. Nor had she seen him on the plane, thanks in part to his window seat and strategic use of newspaper, pillow, grey hair dye and a cane. He gave the cane to a surprised old lady as he came out of customs.

He watched the flat for a long time. No need to check the names in the hallway or get any closer to the building yet. They could do that later. He ground out his cigarette and walked to the travel bureau on the next street, found the owner, and showed his identification.

"Police?" said the woman, startled. But she told him what he wanted to know.

A block away Linnet and Stephen were arguing.

"Did you have to come here so directly?" Stephen demanded. "Anyone could have seen you." He was a slight but muscular man with a deep tan and very blonde hair. Unless you were

75

directly across the table from him, Linnet thought, you would never guess he was over fifty. Well, she too was older than she looked. They were well matched.

"No one knows me, darling," she said.

"You said a woman traced us. Very likely someone knows you quite well. One of your indiscretions?"

"Blaming everything on me again?" she answered. They were at a table near the balcony, at a hurried dinner of cold lobster salad, bread, and wine. The door to the balcony was open and the summer air through the screen blew at the candlelight.

"It's usually your fault," he said amiably. The phone rang and he jumped up.

"Yes?" After a moment he hung up.

"You can have the little boy you wanted," he said.

"What? When?"

"Whenever you like. Tomorrow? It's all arranged."

"But - I just arrived. It's too soon. He'll get in our way."

"You tell me for months that all you want is this particular child and suddenly it's too soon?"

"But Stephen - this one's for me. It's not like the others. I have to be ready for him. Right now it'll get in the way."

"You wanted a kid. They get in the way. Any parent will tell you that. I'll tell you that. He's not staying here."

"Of course. Can't you put it off - another week?"

"Darling, for you," Stephen leaned over the table, "No. I have other things to do. And you'd better find out who sent that woman. I'm sure you can make sure one little boy does not interfere."

"I don't have him yet," she said. "He can't interfere until you get him for me, can he?"

"Not me, said Stephen, raising his glass. "I'm an innocent artist with a little photo shop on the rue de Lausanne. Don't blame me for anything you don't like."

"Of course not, darling." she smiled.

She first met Stephen when she was sixteen, almost by chance when her father came to Europe on one of his frequent business trips. Raised in France and England, her father returned to his native India in 1948 to embrace nationalism and an arranged marriage. Finding political ideals as difficult to embrace as the family he had to live with, he continued to return to Europe as often as he could. Linnet grew up on Indian goods and European ideas. As soon as she was old enough she spent all her holidays traveling with her father. That summer in Geneva he brought her downtown to have her picture taken and there was Stephen behind the camera. She spent much of her time after that, while Father was in his meetings, with Stephen. He gave her a good time and she always liked a good time. Then, shortly before her father had to leave Geneva, Linnet surprised Stephen in his studio. It was a surprise for both of them, and opened up a whole new world that Linnet soon could not let go even if she wanted to. Sometimes Linnet resented this, but most of the time Stephen let her have her own way, and they worked together well, she thought. There were moments, of course. But then, she had learned to take care of herself.

ᶳᵃ

And so, on a hot, dry day in August, little Peter Samuels, age four, went downtown with his mother to buy school clothes, and lost his grip, disappearing into an unusually crowded sidewalk just outside the park. Buses, cars, cabs and motorbikes continued

77

to hurry along the street in their ordered way as pedestrians hurried along beside them on the sidewalk, unhappy with women like Katrien who stopped suddenly, getting in everyone's way, just another foolish mother who didn't have the sense to keep a grip on her child.

She stood silent in the first moments, as the crowds pushed her back and forth, eventually to the edge of the curb. She had done everything Joanne suggested. She had gone with Georges to the police, given over the photo, had the locks changed. Everything except hide in the flat. Everything except move on to another place where they might or might not find her. She was tired of hiding, tired of secrets. She had done everything except explain to Georges why she did not find it as shocking as he did, this thing that was happening to her. She told them the picture was probably taken sometime in the year before she had regained custody, when she thought the children were in Delhi, but Joanne was convinced instead, that it had been taken since they came to Geneva. A specially trained policewoman involved in the investigation wanted to question Arulai too, but Katrien refused. Not that it was too much to think about, that whatever affected Peter might also affect Arulai. She had already been thinking about it. During their first five months in Geneva when they were living with the Streckers, Joanne was more worried than Katrien about Arulai. Arulai would be alright. But Katrien would not have the police questioning her. Joanne never worried about Peter. Only Katrien worried about Peter. And then she took steps to resist. They warned her against resisting. What would they do now?

For the first few moments, standing on the busy sidewalk, she didn't even call Peter's name. What good would it do? But then, feeling she must at least seem to be a good mother, she began to call out and, as she heard her own voice, the fear rose, and she began to cry and scream for him there on the curb.

That night her landlady, invited her to sleep downstairs if she wanted to. Katrien stayed in her own flat but agreed that she and Arulai would at least come down and have breakfast with Mrs. Roberts to prove they were alright. That night she checked the doors three times before she went to bed. Arulai slept with her that night with Christina's crib across the room. They will not drive me from my own apartment, she thought. I will not go back to live with the Streckers. I will learn to be strong, whatever it takes. For my daughters. I will succeed where my mother failed...

❧

She was fifteen, starting at her second boarding school, near Lausanne, when her mother went into the hospital. At first the doctors said she had a nervous breakdown, but after a year she was no better. Whenever her stepfather went to visit, her mother screamed at him as if he was the devil. Once he took Katrien along and she saw for herself. After that, she didn't want to visit her mother and always got stomachaches the day before. Then the doctors said maybe it was a brain tumor, but they were not sure. Katrien threw herself into her studies and tried not to think of her mother. Her stepfather came to take her home for holidays, but she began to feel strange around him, and as often as she could she spent the holidays instead with her school friends and their families. After the spring when she was seventeen, she distanced herself from him as much as she could, so that when her mother died, several years later, she didn't hear about it for a long time; by then her stepfather wasn't sure where

she was. Her mother's will left her a small summer chalet up in
the Jura and some money. She went to a lawyer as soon as she
could and gave the Streckers legal rights to manage the chalet as
they saw fit. She left the money in her stepfather's hands and,
when she realized this and tried to get it, there was nothing left.
He couldn't touch the chalet. Her mother had put it in Katrien
and Arul's names. Maybe she wasn't crazy, after all.

She was still in school when she met Joanne Strecker, in the
spring when she was seventeen. Her class took a trip along the
lake to Geneva, stopping at each of the ancient Roman ruins. By
then her stepfather was living in Geneva and he invited her for
dinner. After dinner he took Katrien and her best friend, Amy,
to one of his friends' parties across the city, in a private mansion
on the waterfront. There was a garden with Roman replicas of
the statues she had seen that day, and a pool with fountains and
night lighting, and everywhere people much older than she, who
looked at her very strangely and said strange things. There were
strange odors and strange things to look at and, although she
usually tried to be as mature and sophisticated as possible, and
perhaps because most of the people were much older than she, it
made her afraid. Her fear began to grow after Amy went off,
laughing, with one of the other guests.

She began to wander through the house to get away from the
strangeness, holding her can of Coke like a security blanket,
looking closely at all the paintings and going into every bathroom
she came to, just for the security of being able to lock the door.
But then she came to a room where she did not realize, until she
shut the door, that she was not alone. She tried to open it again
but they were too quick for her. It was her stepfather with one
of his friends and another woman. She soon began to
understand, after all, why her mother went crazy. They shut her

in the room with them and began to make very strange demands of her. She thought she knew something about adulthood by now, but even so she did not understand.

That night, still in that house, in that room, finally alone, she had a dream. Over and over again she had the sense of being hurled high through the air, thrown from a great distance, from deep inside a lush, green forest. Over and over again, she was hurled past miles of beautiful trees, flying at a speed beyond her control over beautiful gardens far below, and in the end hurled out through a pair of massive, brass-coloured gates which shut behind her with a tremendous crash. She landed against a dry hillock of dust and sand. All around was desert, with low patches of weeds and scrub brush. Above it was a dry, pink sky. All motion had stopped and she was on solid ground. After a long time, she stood up in the dry air and the patch of dusty ground felt solid beneath her feet. The air was warm, and scented faintly with incense. The brass gates hovered far in the distance, quivering in some unseen heat.

'I am east of Eden now,' she thought. Then gradually the gates disappeared and she woke to find herself in that empty room in a grey, cold stillness, with a bad headache.

It was a small narrow room with a high ceiling, the walls painted dark blue, a still room with a large, bare window with a black shade someone had released in the night so it was now nothing but a thin black cylinder high on the wall. The window was curtained only by the leaves from the trees lining the street outside. It was raining.

When she was a very little girl, her father and stepmother sometimes locked her in a bare room without food for a night or a whole day because she was bad. It was always a room with the light switch on the outside and at first they always left the light on. Then once she burnt her hand unscrewing the bulb. They had to take her to the clinic, and the nurses began to ask questions. After that, after her hand healed, they always left the light off when they shut her up in that room. When she woke that morning in Geneva when she was seventeen, the ceiling light was still on, bright, over her head. She was hungry.

Slowly she remembered the world of the night before, as it had flashed before her over and over again. She remembered with a sudden humiliation that she had, that night, against all her better judgement, prayed desperately for help to a god she did not believe in. This was in some ways more troubling than anything else she remembered. At school they made her go to chapel, and there was something about the dusky light and reverberating musical echoes that comforted her, but she had vowed years ago never again to pray. Now she had broken her vow. She was used to others betraying her, she thought. But now she had betrayed herself. For a long time, as she sat and stared at the grey light outside the smeared panes of window glass, she forced herself to remember this and nothing else, as if by thinking about it she could restore her vow to its former wholeness and return to her intentional non-religion, return again through the great gates which had now shut her out. But it was impossible, for this morning, this grey rainy morning when she was seventeen, she realized for the first time in her life that it was not only those who were religious who were cruel.

After a while her head stopped aching a little and she tried the door. It opened. It was still very early. She found her way out of the house without rousing anyone. She saw no one. Out in the street she found some money in her pocket and she took a cab downtown to the spot where her class was to meet for the bus back to school. It was hours too early. The plaza was silent except for the drizzling rain, all the shops shut, and there was nowhere to wait except a small stone church which abutted the plaza. The cab driver waited to see that she could get into the church before he drove away. The door to the church opened easily. She went in, through a dark musty entryway to the sanctuary itself, unlit   From the windows high above her the grey morning light reflected on gold paint around the altar, and two silver candlesticks. Katrien sat in a back pew and waited. After a little while several people came in and a service began. Matins. She knew it from school.

When it was over she stayed, silently, in her pew as everyone left. Then one woman noticed her and came back.

"Excuse me," she said, kneeling in the aisle beside the girl, "Is there something you need help with?" She had a very young face for someone with grey hair. It was a kind, quiet face.

"I'm waiting for my schoolbus," said Katrien. Her head was not so bad now, but she still felt dizzy.

"Do they know you are waiting here for it?" The woman looked down at her as if something was wrong. I probably look terrible, Katrien thought. My hair is all messed up.

"It doesn't come until two o'clock," she said.

"Dear child, it's not even eight in the morning. You can't wait here all that time!" the woman said, staring down at her, alarmed at the girl's passive, patient, empty face. The girl stared at her and slowly remembered the gates banging shut in her dream.

That morning Joanne Strecker took her home, cooked breakfast for her, let her take a shower, lent her some clothes, drove her to the plaza at two o'clock to catch her bus back to school, and didn't ask any questions. Several weeks later Katrien finished school and went to live with the Streckers. Soon after this, through Joanne and Jules and a group of friends in the little stone church, she met Arul. Her stepfather tried to keep in touch but she turned 18 before he found her and she was married before Christmas.   There was nothing about Arul that she had any cause to regret. Because of Joanne and Arul, she need not go crazy, like her mother. Because of the Streckers and Mrs. Roberts, she could now go yet another step and make a haven for her own children, and for her son, when he was found. Whenever he was found. If...

Unbidden, she suddenly remembered the deep rectangular pools of water between the marble pillars at her stepfather's party, so long ago. Had the pools really been that deep or was it a later nightmare? Would they ever find Peter again?

ẽ

When she woke the sun was high and Arulai was sitting, reading a book in a chair across the room. From the crib, Christina was making small but urgent noises, which were quickly accelerating in volume. Katrien pulled herself up and brought the infant back to the bed to feed and change her. Arulai looked up from her book.

"Mama, will they also take Christina away?" she asked. Then it all came back, the night, the rememberings.

"Pray to God they don't," Katrien said.

"Daddy taught me to pray to God," said Arulai, solemnly.

"Do you remember him very well?"

"Yes. I think so. If he was still alive, Mama, would this be still happening to us or not?"

"I don't know," Katrien said, fingering Christina's soft, dusky skin. "I just don't know." It was odd, she thought. There was

84

a certain sense of relief, now that this thing had been done, after so much fear for so long. As if nothing bad could happen to her ever again, now that it was over. But was it?

"What do you think Peter is doing right now, Mama?" Arulai asked.

Katrien shook her head. "Go wash your face and get dressed," she said. "We're going downstairs for breakfast, and you can't wear your pajamas."

Katrien kept her in the house during those first few days after Peter disappeared. For Arulai, however, there was no relief. Whenever the phone rang, Arulai answered it before Katrien. Often Katrien came into the dining room to find Arulai sitting at the front window, peering down into the street, watching for her brother. The two had been together since Peter was born. Arulai's bond with Peter is much closer than mine, thought Katrien. She did not completely understand what was happening - did that make it easier or harder?

"Mama, what will we do now?" Arulai asked after breakfast that first morning, when they were back in their own apartment again. Katrien sat at the dining room table, her work spread out around her. Arulai sat on the couch in the living room, still holding her book.

"What do you mean? I will still do my work and you will still go to school."

"I mean, how will we get Peter back? Is Georges going to help us?"

"He is trying. But it may take a long time."

"You mean, weeks?"

"Perhaps."

"Where is Peter?"

"I wish I knew, honey. I wish none of this was happening."

"Is it happening because of India?"

"What do you mean?"

"I mean, is it because Grandmother still wants Peter but doesn't want me?"

"I don't think so," Katrien said. "Remember when we were at the airport in Delhi before we came here? Your grandfather promised he would make Grandmother understand that it was right for you to be with me."

"I remember," Arulai said. "But Grandmother liked Peter best. She didn't like me - or you."

"Your grandmother was very protective of children," Katrien said. "I think she liked you more than you think. And she would never kidnap Peter."

"Mama," Arulai said, a few minutes later, looking up from her book. "Maybe they are keeping Peter hostage in the cottage."

"What cottage, honey?"

"Here in Switzerland. The one that belonged to you and Daddy."

"The chalet? Why would you think that?"

"Because - I don't know. It's where the babysitter and her friends took us one day when you were in the hospital with Christina. Maybe it was one of Elise's friends who took Peter?"

Katrien looked at her, startled. Arulai sat, cross-legged, on the couch in her stocking feet. "When I was in the hospital?" she asked. "When Christina was born? Joanne's babysitter took you to a chalet?"

"Not *a* chalet, Mama. *Your* chalet. I know, because Uncle Jules told me that was the key. It was the same key Elise gave to her friends." Arulai, who was speaking hesitantly, began to look afraid. "It's not my fault they took the key," she said.

"I'm not blaming you for anything," Katrien answered. "Can you tell me what the chalet looked like?"

Arulai described it. Clearly it was their own chalet, and a recent memory. Katrien and Arul lived there for two years before returning to India but Arulai, who was born in Geneva, only spent her first few months there. Katrien had not gone back since, reluctant to face the power of the happiest memories of her life, those first years with Arul. If Arulai had been there since, it was not with her mother or the Streckers.

"Elise and her friends took you there, both you and Peter?"

Arulai nodded.

"This is important to me, Arulai," Katrien said. "Can you tell me what her friends looked like?"

The girl looked down and frowned, as if trying to remember. "There were two of them," she said. "One was Elise's new boyfriend. He had brown hair. He was very thin. And his uncle. He was older. He drove the car. He was Swiss. He never spoke English. Elise and her boyfriend - they spoke English to us and French to each other."

"Was it Elise's idea to go to the chalet - or did her friends want her to do it?"

"I think it was Elise. One day she told us we were all going - just for fun. I didn't tell her it was our chalet. She didn't know I saw her take the key and give it to them. I pretended I didn't know. She pretended it was a chalet that belonged to her boyfriend."

"Were you there at night or just during the day?"

"Just the day. It was a secret and we had to be back before Joanne so she wouldn't find out. Elise was scared that Joanne would find out and she would get into trouble, and lose her job too. I heard her boyfriend say not to worry about the money - that he would pay her more."

"He said that in English?"

"Well - I guess he said it in French. I understood, but they didn't know. French is easier to understand than it is to speak, you know. And I didn't want them to know I understood."

"Arulai, why didn't you tell me this earlier?"

Arulai looked down at her book. "I don't know," she said. "You're blaming me, aren't you?"

"I'm just worried, not angry. Do you - remember what they did while you were there?"

"Yes, of course I remember. You know Mama, I have a very good memory."

"You have an extraordinary memory," Katrien said. "It worries me sometimes."

"Mama, you worry too much."

"Then tell me - what did you and Peter do that day, in the chalet?"

"We played," the girl answered readily. "They let us climb up into the attic. We drew pictures. We wanted to play outside, but they didn't want us to. They stayed downstairs. They kept arguing. It was all in French, but I didn't understand most of it."

"Did anyone take any pictures?" Katrien asked, as calmly as she could.

Arulai shook her head. "No," she said. "That happened afterwards, I think - the next time Elise came over to babysit. But I wasn't there. Not for the pictures."

Katrien looked at her quickly, then got up from the table to go sit beside her on the couch. She stared over her head out the window until Arulai put her book on the floor and looked up into her face.

"Mama, are you going to cry?"

"No, no," Katrien said. "I'm not going to cry. You know - I think what you're telling me might really help us all find Peter. But you need to tell me more, whatever you remember, even if it seems very strange. You're an important witness, you know. Would you recognize Elise's friends again, if you saw them?"

"Of course. But Mama - do I have to talk to that police lady?"

"No. You don't have to talk to her. I might. I might decide to tell her whatever you tell me. But I promise you won't."

"Good," Arulai said. "She had bad breath. And it wasn't anything really bad that happened, you know. I mean, some things were. Stealing the key - that was bad. And when they let us down out of the attic, they kept looking at me, like they didn't like me. I think they argued because Elise wanted to go home that afternoon and they wanted to stay - or to go somewhere else. But nothing bad happened to us."

"Do you think Elise was afraid - of her boyfriend - or the other man?"

"No. I was, a little, but she wasn't. She liked them. You could tell. Did we almost get kidnaped?"

"Maybe," Katrien said. "Tell me more about the uncle - the man who just spoke French - was it his car?"

"I think so. He drove it. He was strange - he looked at me as if I made him nervous."

"Why would you make him nervous?"

"I don't know. Maybe because I told him off?"

"Told him off? What did you say?"

"In India, Grandmother caught a thief once. I heard her tell him off. So that's how I told this man off. I said, 'You're a bad man if you don't take us home right now! If you hurt me and my brother,' I said, 'my mother will find you wherever you are and get you back for it. You won't escape. She'll curse you until you turn purple and dry up so your eyes are like nuts in your head!' That's what I said. Grandmother cursed the thief with the wrath of Kali, but I didn't know if this man would believe in Kali's wrath. Anyway, I told him off. And he took us home. The others just laughed at me, but he didn't."

"Did he understand you?"

"Oh, yes. He understood everything we all said. He just wouldn't speak English."

"What did he look like?"

Arulai sighed. "So many questions, Mama." she complained.

"Well - one or two more, and then I'll stop. When they took pictures later - can you tell me everything that you remember from that?"

Arulai sighed again. "Yes, Mama," she said in a resigned voice. "That was the next time Elise came over. Maybe it was the next day. We were in the farmhouse. Elise's boyfriend and his uncle came for lunch. Elise got all made up. She said they wanted to take our pictures. But I didn't want to - I mean, I didn't want them to remember what I look like. I wanted them to go away. But they didn't, so I went out to the barn. I told Elise I would tell on her, about the day before, if she made me have my picture taken."

"What about Peter?" Katrien asked. Arulai leaned against her mother and looked at her fingers.

"I wanted to take him out with me, Mama," she said. "But Elise grabbed him and then her boyfriend's uncle grabbed him. They started tickling him so he would stop crying. I ran away then. They never came and looked for me. I stayed out all afternoon. I didn't even go in until I heard Joanne come home."

"Was Elise still there when you went in?"

"No. Just Peter and Joanne."

"Did Peter ever tell you what happened?"

"No. Mama, I don't want to talk about it anymore."

"Fair enough," Katrien put her arm around her. "You're a great witness. You deserve a break. How about a walk down to the patisserie?"

"But what if someone calls about Peter?" Arulai twisted the ring on her mother's finger.

"They'll leave a message. When we come back we can call Georges and ask if he would drive us up into the Jura, maybe tomorrow, to check on the chalet and make sure Peter isn't there. How about that?"

Arulai agreed, reluctantly.

Katrien phoned Joanne later in the afternoon. Yes, the chalet had been vacant at the end of April and beginning of May. It was vacant most of this month, as a matter of fact. Most of the people who looked at it this summer considered it too rustic for comfort. It really did need work. Joanne checked it occasionally. There had been no sign of forced entry or unwelcome visitors. Next, Katrien phoned Georges. He was willing to drive them up the next afternoon. Last of all, when Arulai was in bed, she phoned the police and told them Arulai's story. They decided to check the chalet that night.

She tried to work on her translations. It was hard to concentrate. Between Christina and her work she was eventually able, surprisingly, to block out a certain level of the pain for short periods of time.

Joanne called shortly after midnight. She had met the police at the chalet and gone through it carefully. There was no sign of Peter. There was no reason for Katrien to drive up with Georges,

WATCHMEN OF THE HOUSE

unless she wanted to. In the morning it was Arulai, after all, who insisted.

Georges drove them up after lunch. The chalet was in a small village an hour's drive north along the highway and up into the brown hills along the French border. The house was a peasant's cottage, built long ago in hand-hewn stone, with wooden window frames and shutters painted red and white. It had been in Katrien's mother's family for generations. It was only a short walk from the train station in the village. The small, fenced yard ended in a steep hillside, owned by a nearby farmer, terraced with vineyards which stretched down to the highway, far below. The lake glittered in the distance and beyond it, on clear days, the snow-covered Alps hung low on the Western sky.

It was a clear day. They parked in the small gravel driveway. An old woman in the road called to Katrien. She recognized her, a neighbor, a widow who always seemed to be in the road, or in her front garden, or in the village street gazing in the direction of their cottage.

"Mrs. Boucher!" she called. "How are you?" The old lady hurried volubly over to the gate. Katrien introduced Georges and the children.

"So big now!" Mrs. Boucher said, smiling down at Arulai. "And last time I saw her she looked just like her little sister does - such a beautiful baby, madame. And your husband?"

"I'm sorry, Mrs. Boucher, but my husband died in India."

The woman started, exclaimed, and began to lament, staring at Georges with his priest's collar and more and more curiously at Christina. "And so little!" she said.

"We've come to check on the chalet," Katrien said, interrupting her abruptly. "Has anyone been here recently?"

"Here? The chalet?"

92

"Yes. Have you seen anyone at all - since the middle of last week?"

Last night there was a car, the woman said. Katrien said yes, she knew about that. But before that? Before that? No, Mrs. Boucher had not seen anyone before that. This was as good as a guarantee that no one had been there.

They talked for a few more minutes. Katrien asked about other neighbors she remembered. When they parted, the old lady hurried home to get her shopping basket and was soon hurrying down the road to the village.

"Do we still need to go inside, Mama?" Arulai asked.

"I want to," Katrien said, "But you don't have to. Do you want to play outside while we look around?"

"No. I want to be with you."

"Good," Katrien said, looking at Georges. "Even if she seems to be a half mile down the road, Mrs. Boucher will notice exactly how many of us go inside, and how long we stay." There was an edge to her voice.

"You are worried," Georges said, "But I do not think you are so worried about the village gossip, are you?"

The shutters were shut and the cottage was dark and stuffy. Katrien switched on the lights as they went from one small room to the next, then down into the cellar. Georges pulled down the ladder from the trap door in the hall ceiling, and climbed up into the loft room above. He found nothing. Arulai went up after him and they let her play up there while they looked through the rest of the small cottage. The walls were bare except for some ancient lithographs from the years when it was last decorated, shortly after the first world war. The furniture was all worn down, the beds musty, a few chairs badly scratched and the kitchen stove needed to be scoured. No wonder Joanne rented it so cheaply. New mattresses and a few new lamps and layers of paint might help, at the very least. But there was no sign of any recent disorder, or anything unusual.

"I'm sorry if I wasted your time, coming here," Katrien said to Georges as she returned to the foot of the ladder in the hall. She called up to Arulai to come down.

"Looking for lost sheep is part of my calling," he said, as he went past her into the front room to look closer at the framed pictures by the door. If the shutters were open, this would be the brightest room of the cottage in spite of its dark wooden walls. Next to the pictures was a built-in bookcase and Georges began to look through the remaining books. For the most part they were dusty and leather-bound, some with still-gilded edges, some eaten by years of neglect, others falling apart from much use, with a few more recent paperbacks here and there, perhaps left by seasonal tenants who came for an inexpensive ski vacation or school holiday, or else those willing to live a very simple life during a semester at one of the colleges in Geneva. Most of the books were in English or French, but a few were in German and, to his surprise, Georges found a Greek New Testament pushed way in the back on a high shelf.

"Was there a theologian in your mother's family?" he called.

"What? Arulai, come down, please. We have to go home." Katrien turned from the tiny ladder and looked in the door to the front room. "A theologian?"

"Someone left a Greek New Testament here," He held it up and opened it, gently.

. "Maybe a hundred years ago. The chalet belonged to my mother's grandparents."

Georges looked down at the title page. It was exactly ten years since the book in his hand was printed. There was a name penned on the front page in a small, neat hand.

"No one more recently," he asked lightly.

"No. No theologians. Arulai!"

Arulai's feet were visible at the top of the hole in the ceiling. "Mama," she called. "I found the pictures we drew, that I told you about. But I'm afraid to come down the ladder by myself. Will you come get me?"

"What? What did you find?"

"Just these," She handed a thick pad of loose sheets down through the square trap door. "Mama, will you help me get down? It's scary. I don't want to come down by myself. I can't."

Georges caught the notebook as it tumbled down into his hands, bringing dust down with it on all of them. Christina sneezed as Georges put the pad down and climbed the ladder to reach for Arulai and guide her feet onto the narrow rungs. Christina began to cry and Katrien settled into a chair in the kitchen and began to feed her. When Georges came in and realized she was breastfeeding the baby, as invisibly as this process was taking place, he awkwardly turned his back on her and began to remove the children's drawings from the sketchbook and lay them out on the kitchen table. She is a wonderful woman, he said to himself. Suddenly he realized, startled, that what he meant was only that she was a wonderful mother. Didn't he?

"Mama, did I really look just like Christina when I was little, like Mrs. Boucher said?" Arulai asked some time later, after she told Georges all the stories about each picture. Georges was holding up the drawings against a bright light.

"You did," Katrien said, absently, looking into the cupboards along the wall, Christina, now contented, nestled against her shoulder. "You looked just like your father." Immediately she wished it could be unsaid.

"But Mama, Fiona said my father can't be Christina's father because my father was dead for over three years before Christina was even born."

Katrien focussed deliberately on the chipped, ancient mugs and stoneware within the dark cupboards. "You tell Fiona to mind her own business."

"But Mama - is it true what Fiona said?" Arulai walked around the kitchen as she talked, looking into the lower cabinets and cupboards.

"Arulai," said Georges. "Come tell me about this picture again."

"In a moment," Katrien said to him. "First let me have a talk with this child about when she ought to ask what sort of questions. Arulai, come into the front room for a short - private - talk."

"No, I want to stay in here with Georges and talk," The girl grabbed his arm. He took her hand and looked down at her. Above his collar, his face was still red from the heat of the cottage. He looked, very slightly, fierce.

"If your mama wants to have a talk with you, I think you need to do what she says," he advised. Arulai complied, slowly and reluctantly, and went out into the hall ahead of her mother.

"Thank you," Katrien said to him. He didn't answer.

When they came back a few minutes later, Arulai was quieter. She helped Georges put the pictures back into a stack. They were ordinary drawings. One had Peter's name on it.

"I wrote that for him. See - here? He tried to copy it. But he wasn't very good."

"What did you do with the crayons?" Katrien asked.

"I put them in the fire."

"You had a fire in the attic?"

"No, I mean later. Peter didn't want the crayons anymore so I put them in the fire. Will we live here now, Mama?"

"No, I don't think so, honey. Maybe someday, but not for a while." She noticed Georges had taken the Greek New Testament off the bookshelf.

"A loan?" he asked, quietly.

"Of course," she answered. "You can have it if you like."

"Good!" said Arulai. "That means Peter can come home to Mrs. Roberts' house and live in a place he feels safe, right Mama?" She followed them out to the car, trailing the wooden walls with her fingers. Outside Katrien looked at Georges, this balding, shy priest who continued to surprise her with his perceptive silence. He smiled and opened the car door. I think he is going to cry, she thought.

"Yes, honey, we certainly want Peter to feel safe." she answered.

Powers

ॐ

Midmorning on a Saturday several weeks later, Timothy Green and a tall girl with dark, shoulder-length hair and deep grey eyes got out of a train at Lausanne and walked down the steep, cobbled lane to the quay and the path along the beach, leading up the lake. They each lit a cigarette and the ashes occasionally dropped into the sandy earth at their feet. The girl wore a short, printed sundress and sandals, and carried a large black leather shoulder bag with a cream sweater hanging out one end. They walked slowly, talking at length, gradually making their way up the beach toward the ancient castle built on a protruding rock a half mile up the beach from Lausanne. On their right the lake glittered with sun and the flags from a dozen sailboats. The peaks of the Dents du Midi far above on the other shore were still wreathed in icy mist and clouds despite the sun and warmth of the August day. They stopped once to get a lemonade and now and then to take photographs of one another against the backdrop of the lake, or else against the steep, vivid green of the facing hills which threaded up into the mountains on the left, the narrow pass of highway like a faint grey thread cut through the green. They walked like people comfortable with one another, not concerned with impressing each other; they knew one another too well for that.

Timothy did not expect to see Thad Hoskins standing in line ahead of them when they arrived at the drawbridge of Chillon castle to buy tickets and guidebooks. When he saw him, he swore.

"What's the matter?" asked the girl.

"That bloke up there in the shiny white sneakers."

"He looks harmless."

"He's a damn pest. One of those sincere missionary sorts. He's sure to come crashing into us somewhere in the castle. How about lunch first?"

"Don't be silly. Besides, I think he sees you."

He had indeed. With a word to a small group of smiling faces in t-shirts who stood around him, Thad gave up his place in line and pushed back through the crowd to Timothy and the girl.

"Just lovely," Timothy swore under his breath. "Thad, old man!" he said aloud. "Fancy meeting you here."

"I thought it was you," Thad said with a smile, holding out his hand. Timothy, then the girl, shook it.

"This is Anne," said Timothy.

"Hello. Isn't this wonderful," said Anne cheerfully. "Are you one of Timothy's friends?

"Years ago," Timothy said quickly. "Come up to see the historic sights for the day, have you?"

"Yes," said Thad. "I brought a group of visiting students from the church. You know, they have good concerts here at night. There's one tonight, in fact."

The line moved quickly and they bought their tickets and went in through the guard-house to the walled-in fortress, built between 800 and 1300, with its battlements, shops, dungeons, towers and window boxes.

"Church? Are you a priest?" Anne asked. Timothy prodded her.

"I'm just a part-time preacher," said Thad. "I work with an Indian missionary group, in the office in Geneva."

"How exciting," said Anne. "Have you been to India, then?" Timothy prodded her again, but instead of taking the hint she took his hand. Resigned, he swung his camera over his shoulder, leaned against her, and sighed.

"Yes," said Thad. "I was there until Christmas. But a girl who came to us was killed and they decided it was time for a change in the organization, so they moved me here. Waste of money if you ask me. Did you get one of those guides?"

"Oh yes," said Anne. "How terrible that must have been for you, having someone killed. What happened?" Timothy put his arm around her shoulder and started to study the guidebook.

"Damn, Annie - you got a German one. They have it in six languages. Couldn't you get one in English or French?"

"We can exchange it," she said. "I wasn't paying attention. I went to India once - on a tour," she said to Thad. "I got very sick. You have to be careful what you eat, don't you?"

"You get used to it."

"Why did that girl get killed?" Anne repeated, ignoring Timothy's attempts to move her away from Thad, across the stone street and toward the first door into the castle.

"Jill? No one really knows. It was strange. None of us were expecting her. You know, I really shouldn't neglect my friends," He pointed to a small group of people behind him. "They're Americans, only here for a few weeks. They wanted to see something 'really old.'" The group of Americans in t-shirts hovered in the background. "I'm sure we'll meet each other again, inside," he said. "Maybe we can chat later on."

"Of course," Anne said.

"You don't want to neglect your friends," Timothy agreed.

It was after they got the English guidebook and went in through the cool stone doorways up to the second floor that Timothy suddenly stopped abruptly on the stairs and stared at the dim, cool stone. Through a tiny hole in the battlement wall he could still see Thad chattering with his group in the courtyard below. Anne turned around when he didn't follow her up the stairs.

"Is something wrong?" she asked.

He stared up at her. "What did he say was the name of that girl?"

"I don't know." She thought for a moment. "Something like Jill, I think. Why? An old girlfriend?"

Timothy didn't answer, but started, slowly, up the stairs toward her. "How would you know a missionary in India?" she asked. He still didn't answer but followed her silently through the first few rooms and into the great hall, where the walls were painted red and white in a herringbone pattern common during and after Charlemagne's era.

"Damn," he said.

"You're moody all of a sudden. How do you know him, anyway?"

"We were at school," he answered in a dull voice. "Then he came into the shop one day and remembered me, blast him. You're sure he said Jill?"

"You want to go ask him? You weren't very interested in talking to him a few minutes ago."

"He's a cursed nuisance."

"Ooh, nasty. I think he's cute."

"And I thought you had good taste."

"Well, don't worry. I'm sure we'll see him again in here somewhere. The castle is not that big."

They wandered through the great hall, examining the tapestries and wooden benches, climbing the stone steps under each window to look out through the large, lattice frame. The castle was begun in Frankish times and Anne followed the historical notes carefully.

"I wonder if even the plants are historically accurate," she said. "Switzerland was not even a federated group of states when the castle was begun."

"If it was, they wouldn't have needed a castle," said Timothy. He had his camera out by now and filled his time, silently, taking pictures, changing film several times.

They met Thad and his friends again in the dungeon, where Thad was searching, like a good tourist, for Lord Byron's graffiti. Anne found it first, and read part of Byron's poem about Chillon out of a book she'd brought.

"You know, Hoskins," said Timothy as casually as he could, after Anne read the poem, "What did you say was the name of that girl in India?"

"Girl? What girl?"

"The one you mentioned outside. Who died."

"Oh, yes. Johnson. Jill Johnson. There was some talk about whether that was really her name, but that's what she called herself. I never met her, you know. I got a letter about her coming, the day she arrived, and then I saw her body after she was dead. Why?"

"Jill Johnson? Are you sure?"

"You look a bit upset about it, Green," Thad said. "Did you know her?" Timothy was squinting at him. Anne was in a distant corner, examining methods of torture.

"Yeah," Timothy said after a long time, and with some effort. "Yeah, I knew her. You say she's dead?"

"She is indeed. I'm sorry."

"What happened to her?"

"That's what everyone wanted to know. They said she died in an alley about two in the morning. But no one could suggest why, or even why she had come to India, since the letter I got turned out to be a fake. Green - are you going to be alright?"

"Yes," Timothy looked around wildly, staring at the wall nearest the pillar where Byron had scratched his name. Anne came back to them and he stared at her like some stranger. "Yes, yes, yes. I'll be just fine," he said.

"Tim!" Anne reached over to him. "What happened?"

"Nothing, love," said, smiling bleakly. "Just a moment of dizzy. I'll be fine in no time."

"What happened?" she demanded of Thad. Her grey eyes flashed at him.

"I'm afraid I gave him some sudden bad news," he apologized.

"He asked about that girl."

"Yes."

"How would he know her?" she demanded.

"He hasn't told me."

"Leave me alone," said Timothy to Thad. "Just take your fun little group of Americans and go away and leave me alone. You are the most disgusting bastard I ever met."

"Tim!"

"And leave Anne alone," he added. "How do I know you won't kill her, too?"

"Good heavens."

"Tim, you're being very unkind," Anne said.

"And he deserves every bloody word of it."

"Look," Thad pulled a card out of his shirt pocket and scribbled on it. "Here's my address. If you want to talk about it, come see me, will you? They're still investigating her death. Maybe you can help, Green. You're the first person I've met who even knew her. You could help her a lot by telling the police whatever you know."

"Police?" Timothy stood up and took Anne's arm. "What would I want with the police? They can't help her very much if she's dead, can they?"

Thad looked at him, startled.

"You don't want to help the police?" he asked.

"Come on, Tim," Anne said, pulling him away. "I want to see the rest of the castle."

When Thad saw them again, across a courtyard a little while later, Anne was talking in a steady, animated way into Timothy's ear.

*

Near dusk that evening in Geneva, a dark-skinned man in jeans and gold-rimmed glasses stepped out of Nefertiti's, the Egyptian restaurant on the rue Maunoir. Nefertiti's catered chiefly to Islamic residents who followed the Prophet's injunction against alcohol, but whether its clients heeded the Prophet in their private lives or not, the prices were good and the food tolerable. Many of Geneva's foreigners found their way to Nefertiti's.

As the heavy beat of Egyptian music faded gradually behind him, he turned up the street and followed the narrow brick sidewalk to the neat brick buildings of homes and private flats further up, in the cool night. Eventually he stopped to light a cigarette in a recessed doorway opposite a group of ancient, narrow stone houses, private townhouses dating back to the fifteenth and sixteenth century, renovated to give their present owners the greatest possible comforts of life in Geneva's old city. Leaning against the dark wall, he stood there for a long time, watching. The evening was grey by now and the dark brick of the buildings like mottled smoke, their dull red slate roof tiles far above darkening the evening sky.

He lit another cigarette, then another. People passed by in the night along the narrow street and narrower sidewalk. Now and then a small car hurried along the incline.

A small, bulky, clean-shaven man in a dark suit came along the street, whistling and carrying a briefcase. He looked over for a moment at the figure in the doorway as he reached for his house key. People often stood in the doorways on summer nights in this section of town, especially the foreigners who were accustomed to do it in their own country. Georges had a sense for people, and he did not sense any danger from this odd dark man in gold glasses and a silver watch who stood across the street, smoking a cigarette as Georges reached for his key. He turned his back on him and went in, so preoccupied with his own thoughts that a moment later he was hardly aware that the encounter had taken place at all.

The man watched until lights came on in the second floor flat, then he looked up to the top floor, above it, and pulled on his cigarette. The windows were open in the front room of the top flat and lace curtains moved in and out with the evening breezes. Somewhere in the flat there was a light on, but not at the front of the house. After a long time the man ground out the cigarette against the cement wall and strode away, quickly, unaware that behind the lace curtains Katrien was watching him go.

She had been looking out the window at the street when he first appeared at the corner and she stared, squinting in the evening light until he came into the doorway across the street. Then she was sure that it was him. She hovered, like the evening breeze, back and forth between wanting to call out and wanting to retreat and remain unseen. What was Willi doing here? Here, and not in India? And why would he watch her flat like this? Was something else wrong? After he was gone, she sat on the couch and stared into the night for a long time, until Christina began to cry and Arulai came in from the yard. She passed through the dark room toward the lighted kitchen to make dinner.

After he reached the foot of the hill, Willi got into a small black car and drove north along the neck of Leman, north following the highway as far as Nyon, then turning down the narrow streets and into the lanes behind it which led to the villages and private homes. He turned the car down a long driveway and pulled up in front of an old farmhouse with a brick barn and enclosed stone wall around the yard. A dog came out, barking at him from the gate. Behind him a man followed from the barnyard in a grubby shirt and old khaki pants with dusty rubber boots, all colorless in the encroaching night. As he passed under the light by the gate Willi could see that he was very tall, with greying hair and a craggy face. His old clothes hung on him with a baggy distinction most commonly seen among the rich who wore old clothes because they could afford to do anything they liked.

"Hello!" the man called out.

"I'm looking for Jules Strecker."

"You've found him."

"Willi Samuels."

"Oh yes," Jules wiped his forehead with an ancient rag, then stuffed it into his back pocket. "You're the man the police were going to send. Good. Come on through the gate. Don't mind the dog." They shook hands and Willi followed a pebbled path through a dense growth of low bushes. "The papers are in the house," Jules said. "Come on in. I was just taking care of some things in the barn. We run a small farm when we aren't doing international business. It keeps us sane. Forgive my ragged appearance."

Jules took off his boots in the doorway and put on an old pair of clogs, motioning Willi inside and turning on more lights. The farmhouse had been completely renovated on the inside and was furnished sparely. The dog's feet clicked against the shiny black and white marbled tile floors as it followed them into a bright room with couches and a fireplace, around a large, red Persian rug.

"Have a seat," said Jules. "Can I get you a cold beer?"

"Yes, thanks."

"My wife should be home soon. She can tell you more than I about this. I'll get the papers if you can wait a moment." He disappeared through a low doorway and Willi heard several doors opening and closing. Shortly Jules returned with a large manila envelope and put it down, along with a bottle of beer on a small glass table in front of Willi. Willi opened the envelope and pulled out a thick wad of papers, dense with writing. It was thin, cheap copy paper and the writing was only on one side of each sheet.

"It's in Urdu?" Willi said, surprised.

"Yes," Jules sat in a tall, thickly padded wingback chair across from him. There was the sound of another car in the driveway. "That'll be Joanne. Yes, it's Urdu. But it's not. Or so we were told when we found a translator."

"How did you get this?"

"A girl came to us one day. She said she found it in her father's papers, and she wanted to know what it was. She was afraid he would miss it, so she made a copy. That's another copy. At the moment the police have the original. They're hard at work on it tonight, as a matter of fact."

"And you agreed to do a translation?"

"Not at first. She's a popular model, or so my wife says, but her father is in banking. I thought the story was strange and my only available Urdu translator at the time was working on a large project with a tight deadline. But she left it with us, and gave me a very generous advance for translation. It seemed so odd I haven't even processed her cheque."

"When did she bring it to you?"

"Early in June. Two months ago. Ah, Joanne," Jules stood up as his wife came in. "This is Willi Samuels. The man from the Indian police about the Urdu papers."

Joanne Strecker was a slight woman who had always been a little nearsighted, and even after she began to wear contacts she still squinted slightly with a worried look most of the time. In contrast to her husband, she was dressed in low heels and a bright dress, and her hair was pulled back in a loose, very neat chignon.

"How do you do?" she said. "I've just come from dinner with a new client - we got the contract, Jules. Are you all set with something to drink? Good. And you've seen the papers? Good. Let me run and change while you talk. There's some cake and fruit in the kitchen. Would you like anything?"

"Thank you. I just had dinner."

"So," Jules went on after she left. "I let it sit in the files for several months. She called me once or twice, but she didn't seem concerned about the delay. She just wanted to make sure I still had it."

"You knew her before she came in?"

"No, I'd seen her picture in these magazines, you know, and I knew her father's name. To tell you the truth, he is a very well respected banker in Geneva, and I was not sure I ought to be translating his private papers simply at his daughter's request, however strange she found them."

"But you did," said Willi.

"Well- Joanne can tell you that part. We work with publishers, usually, translating published material into other languages for sale and export. We are basically contractors. We provide the translation and our clients take it from there. We do some bits of translating now and then for individuals who come in with personal papers or letters, but there is very little money in it. This is a multi-lingual country, after all, and usually one of your neighbors can translate a letter or two. We contract out to individuals who do the translations for us, and I usually make sure I have at least two or three in any given language so I can double check that a translation is competent before I send it back. Urdu is not a language we have many requests for, and my other Urdu translators were out of the country for various reasons."

There were steps in the hall and Joanne joined them, now in old clothes which nearly matched her husband's, and Birkenstocks.

"So how did you discover that it was 'Urdu but not Urdu'?" Willi asked.

"Yes," Joanne sat down. "That was almost an accident. One of our Hindi translators came in one day and found it in the files.

Urdu is basically a dialect of Hindi that uses the Arabic and Persian alphabets - well, you would know that better than I - and I didn't know he could read Urdu. Most people don't read both, you know. 'Oh, can you read that?' I asked him. He was looking at it with some interest. He's a Swiss whose father was in the Embassy in Delhi for years, and he grew up there. 'Well,' he said, 'this is very strange. It's not Urdu at all, but English with Urdu letters!'"

Willi picked up the papers and flipped through them. Most of them appeared to be lists with text and numbers, and an occasional memo format. There were also several pages of densely written text.

"Well, I don't read Urdu either," he said. "What is it?"

"That was our question." Jules went on. "We decided to have it translated at least to quell our own curiosity. I thought that if the police should get involved, it was time we know about it. The girl kept calling, a little more urgently. Apparently, she said her father discovered the duplication, and she wanted the originals back. Nick, our translator, was as curious as we were at that point, and he produced a translation - transliteration is more correct - within a few days. We just got it yesterday."

"It's a documented list," Joanne said, carefully, "of children for sale, and prices. It has names, addresses, parent's names, private contact phone numbers, in India and four other countries, including Switzerland and Holland. We contacted the police immediately. They said there was a new project in India to stop the sale of children, and recover children who had disappeared, and that you were currently working with them right now, and they would send you over. It is hard to tell where it is based, but the use of Urdu to make notes in English suggested some connection with India and that region of the world, and there are a number of Indian contacts on the list."

"And the banker?"

"We've left that up to the police."

"I see there are five or six pages of text, rather than lists or numbers."

"Oh, yes," Joanne said. "That's apparently a draft of the sort of copy they would circulate to interested clients. It shocked all of us. Here - I think there's an English translation with it - at the bottom? That pile of clipped papers?"

Willi found it and read it silently.

"I've seen this sort of trash before," he said. "At least it makes it quite clear what they are doing."

"Your name is Samuels?" Joanne said, looking at him curiously all of a sudden. "I have a friend - Katrien Samuels. She's one of our translators - a Western woman who married an Indian. I wonder if you are any relation?"

"Yes," Willi said in a distracted way, studying the sheets in front of him. Old Harish's name was on it. Good. It was about time to get that snake into a corner. "She married my brother."

"Oh! Do you know her son disappeared?"

"What?"

"Two weeks ago. She's been very upset. They were downtown and someone grabbed him in a crowd. I wonder if there is any connection - not with you, but with this - " she pointed to the papers.

"Is his name on the lists of children?" Willi asked.

"I don't know - there's an English copy of everything in that clipped pile."

"No," said Willi, a few minutes later. "His name is not here. But you suspect there is a connection?"

"Yes, I do. You're Arul's brother?"

He looked up, surprised. "You knew Arul?"

"Yes. He came to our church when he was studying in Geneva. In fact, we introduced him to Katrien."

"Is that so?" he said, pulling out a cigarette. "Do you mind?"

"No, of course. Does she know you're here? She has not mentioned you - at least not since she came back from India last December."

"No, she doesn't know," he said. "And I'd rather you didn't tell her. I'm afraid I can't say why, except that it has to do with my work. What are you going to do about the banker's daughter?"

"We're still putting her off," Jules said. "She's coming in on Monday and the police are sending two men to the office to meet her and question her there. They didn't want to set off anything premature that might close up some operations by summoning her this weekend."

"Her father may deny everything," Willi said.

"I think you're right," said Joanne. "You know, I sometimes wonder if she's telling us the truth. More likely she stole it from a boyfriend and decided to try and get her father into trouble instead. I can't imagine her father keeping compromising papers of any kind in a place his daughter would find them. He's a very shrewd man. Probably a bit of a strict father, too."

"There's a lot of money involved," Willi peered through the pages of lists in the translation. "And it's all very clearly organized. I suspect this is a much bigger system than I thought."

"Yes, that's what we thought, too," said Joanne. "The quicker it is out of our hands, the better. But I hope you can find Peter Samuels. He was one of the most charming little boys

I've ever seen. They all lived here with us through the winter, until Katrien could get her own apartment."

"So you knew the children?" said Willi. "How did they seem to you, when they first came?"

Joanne peered at him with her worried face, as if trying to read how much he knew, and how much she could tell him.

"They seemed fine," she said. "Why?"

"You probably knew they were with their grandparents, not with Katrien, for almost three years? Katrien finally got custody - my father helped her. I wondered how she would manage, after so long without them."

"She is managing very well," said Joanne, a little sharply. "And she does excellent translation work, too. Peter needed his mother, after so long. I had hoped these papers might help you find him. You are sure his name is not there? It would have been before he disappeared, of course, but they seem to plan some of these things quite far in advance."

"Can I take the papers with me?"

"Yes, please. We want them out of our hands," said Jules.

"Then I'll look through them more carefully later. Why did you expect Peter's name would be here? Was there anything that made you suspect they were targeting him in particular?"

Joanne hesitated, and looked at Jules. He looked back at her steadily.

"My wife is very loyal to Katrien," he said. "She is something like a daughter to us, you see. I think Joanne feels that you ought to ask Katrien and not us, as a third party."

"You see," his wife interrupted. "I know what she went through after Arul died. I heard that his family did not trust her to care for her own children. It was cruel."

"And I am part of that family." Willi said.

113

"Exactly. And what happened to Peter could have happened to anyone. She is not at fault for it in any way. But it may not seem that way to you, if only because your family had already considered her incompetent. Perhaps that has changed. But she is not responsible for Peter's disappearance. She has been very protective of them."

"So, what happened that made you suspect this - " Willi indicated the papers, "might include Peter's name?"

"Oh, yes," said Joanne. "It was a photograph." She told him about it. "We don't know how it was taken. But it was done since they came to Geneva last December. Children develop quickly at that age, you know. And there was a scratch on his arm that I remembered. You'd hardly notice it if you didn't know. But they were here, in the farmhouse, all that time. Someone did it while they were here. That's what no one understands."

"Are either of you photographers?" he asked.

"You mean, is the equipment around the house?" Jules said. "Nothing special. A couple of old Nikons."

"Nothing that would make that sort of photo," said Joanne. "It's a studio quality. She went to the police with it immediately. I'm sure you can check with them. They have it. It may have happened in April. Katrien was in the hospital several times then, and again in early May. Jules was in New York and so I had a babysitter come in several days. It is the only thing we can think of."

"Hospital?" Willi asked. "Is she not well?"

"She's fine," Joanne said carefully. "To be honest, you know, I have heard that she and you did not get along - apart from the family difficulties."

"So she has talked about me."

114

"In the past. We always wrote very regularly. I really think that, where it concerns Katrien, it would be more appropriate for you to contact her yourself, unless it relates to these papers and this investigation. I mean, we are very happy to cooperate with you on this, but - well, I hope you can try and understand."

"Yes, of course," he said. "But as you say, it may relate."

"So you should contact her," Joanne insisted. "Especially if she needs police protection."

"And why would she need police protection?" Willi asked.

❧

Thad shared a small flat with two other men from PUCHSA. It served as a transitional flat for many missionaries who came to visit, or waited to go out to India, or home on furlough. As a result, it had an appearance not unlike a train station, with bare floors and worn down furniture. Books were piled in every corner, no one sure who owned them. The curtains were dusty because the windows were usually open, no one thinking to shut them, and there were two or three posters taped up on bare walls, but no other attempts at decoration. Occasionally someone would clean the kitchen if it began to smell, but the rest of the flat was untouched, and the odour of old sweaters and unwashed sheets hung over it like the perpetual cloud by the ghats in Banaras where they burned corpses.

Thad got home from Lausanne long after midnight, catching a late train and then walking through Geneva in the dark because the buses had stopped running for the night. He was washing up in the bathroom when he heard a loud crashing bang against the front door. It was almost two by now and his flatmates were asleep. The crash came a second time.

115

WATCHMEN OF THE HOUSE

He ran to the door, a towel still in his hand. The noise
would wake up all his neighbors. He pulled the door open, just
as Timothy began to bang against it again, instead this time
crashing his full weight into Thad.

"Let me in you bloody bastard!" he said, the smell of drink
heavy on him.

"Green! What do you think you are doing?" Thad was
forced back with Timothy into the living room, with Timothy
standing there in the middle of the room, regaining his balance.
Anne came in behind Timothy a bit hesitantly and shut the door.
She had on the same sundress she wore earlier in the day, and a
thick Irish knit sweater around her shoulders. She smiled vaguely
at Thad.

"He insisted," she said softly. "I couldn't leave him like this.
Sorry it's so late. Did we wake you?"

"I just came in. He's going to wake up my flatmates. Bit
late for a visit, old man, isn't it?"

"Listen to me," Timothy took him by the shoulders, "What
did you do to Jill? What happened when she went out there? I'll
show you what I think of you." He tried to hit Thad again, but
missed and fell back into the threadbare, but well padded, ancient
couch behind him.

"You listen to me, Green," said Thad, rubbing his shoulder.
"You're welcome here, but you've got to promise to be quiet. I
live with two other people who are asleep in the other room. If
they wake up, they will throw you out. They don't know you
and they won't know that you're not going to hurt anybody. Do
you understand? I don't want to throw you out. I will if I have
to, but I don't want to. Do you want some coffee?"

"Blasted coffee," said Timothy. "Give me something to
drink."

"Milk or coffee. That's all I've got. We're even out of tea at the moment, if you can believe it."

"Milk or coffee," Timothy mimicked, rubbing his fingers through his hair. "What do you drink baby food for?"

"Anne, could you get him a cup of coffee?" Thad asked, pointing to the kitchen. "It's leftover, but it's still warm. Now Green, you were going to come here if you wanted to tell me about Jill Johnson. Was it you who sent her to me in Banaras?"

"And you killed her, you bastard," Timothy tried to get up, but the couch was dated from those years in the early 1970's when couches were notoriously hard to get out of. He sank back against the cushion.

"Green," Thad said, sitting down on the couch beside him. "Listen to me. Somebody shot her through the head with a gun at close range. Do you really think I would do something like that?"

"Shot her," Timothy stared at him, "Shot her through the head with a gun?" he mumbled.

"Yes."

"Shot her?" he echoed. "Bang Bang." He put his fingers to his head, bleakly. "You shot her?" he started to cry, looking at Thad reproachfully.

"No," Thad said. "Somebody else did. We want to know who it was. But first we want to know why she was there. Somebody forged a letter to me from Paul - you remember Paul? It said she was coming. But Paul didn't write it. Maybe you did?"

"Paul? I don't remember any Paul. Small Paul."

"That's just what you always called him. He was a big man. Remember him? He got a bit angry at you a couple of times before he finally asked you to leave. Like the time you forged one of his cheques for a box of cigarettes - and thought you got away with it, remember? You could forge his name on a typed letter, I think. You could forge a whole letter. But that means you also stole some of his stationary. You planned this, didn't you?"

"Such a long time ago, and you dig it up now?" Timothy said. "Don't know what you're talking about. Paul never got angry at me. Nobody ever gets angry with me. I'm a good guy. I even like little children and they like me. Annie can tell you that. I even like Annie. She's pretty hard to like, sometimes, you know."

She came in just then with a tray of steaming coffee. "I made it fresh," she said. "I want a cup myself." She poured Timothy a half cup and then sat down next to him with a full mug for herself. "We've been in that cafe for hours." She had pulled her hair back with a ribbon and had large gold hoops in her ears. Her bare legs stretched out in front of her, lean and bronze from the summer sun.

"Look at it!" Timothy gazed into his cup. "She won't even give me a full cup!"

"You're drunk. You'd spill it."

"You're not so sober yourself," he answered.

"At least I know it," she said.

"I know it too," he said, pushing her, so her coffee spilled on the couch.

"Behave yourself," she said. "Why didn't you tell me you were ever in India?"

"Why should I tell you? I was just a slave working for this bastard and all his little missionary men. Can you believe, Annie, they don't think women are equal. You wouldn't like it at all."

"And who was Jill?" she asked. "One of those unequal women?"

"Unequal? No - who said that? She was equal as they come. A good bugger, she was," said Timothy. "You know," he added slowly, "Somebody shot her through the head. Did you know that?"

"Is it true?" she asked Thad.

"Yes," he said. "At the moment, it's the only thing we're sure about. And I don't think Green is going to tell us very much tonight."

"What do you mean?" Timothy demanded. "I'm talking, aren't I? If I was drunk, I couldn't be talking to you so coherently."

"So, how did you know Jill, old man?"

"Why, she - in front of a lady you want me to tell you?" he said in a stage whisper, glancing from Anne to Thad.

"I think Anne can handle it," Thad said, solemnly. "Can't you, Anne?"

"Absolutely," she said.

"Well, I'm not sure I can," said a voice in the doorway. A young man stood in his underwear, his head closely shaven, old wire framed glasses magnifying pale, bleary eyes. "I have a sermon to preach in the morning, and I would like to get some sleep. Do you know how much noise you are making?" He had a squeaky voice which was even squeakier because he had just woken from a sound sleep.

"Sorry, Jim," said Thad. "Company I wasn't expecting. We'll try to keep it down."

"Yes, minister, we will," said Timothy in a loud voice, trying to salute Jim.

"Shh." said Anne. Jim glanced at her long, bare legs and fled back to his bedroom.

"Now, where were we?" said Timothy.

"Talking in front of a lady, I think," Thad said patiently.

"Yes, do you think it's right?"

"Look, Tim," Anne said. "He wants to know about this girl, Jill. She was one of your girlfriends, wasn't she? It's okay. You can tell us."

"No," he said. "She wasn't."

"What was she then?"

"She was my - fiancée."

"Your fiancée? You mean, somebody you were going to marry?" she asked.

"Yes," he mumbled. "And then he shot her through the head."

"And you just found out today that she was dead?" she asked, incredulous.

"Yes," he started to cry again.

"Green, it happened a year ago," Thad said. "Where did you think she was all this time?"

"And what am I, if she was your fiancée?" Anne demanded.

Timothy looked at her with a hurt expression. "It was a year ago, Annie, like he said. You don't expect me to be celibate for a whole year do you, waiting for my blasted fiancée?"

"You're pretty drunk, aren't you?" she said.

"Don't be ridiculous!" he shouted.

"Why did Jill go to India?" Thad said in a quiet voice. "And why did you forge that letter, Green?"

"Tricked you, didn't I?" said Timothy, more softly. "Tricked you pretty good. Old, naive, innocent little Thad. That cheque of Paul's was just practice. Small stuff. What did I care about money? Still don't care about money. Would be nice if I did sometimes, you know? But it's just too much trouble, worrying about money all the time. I always wanted to trick you. Hated you, I did. I got you back, didn't I? Until you killed her." He looked puzzled. "Why'd you do it, old man?" he said in a surprised voice.

"Someone else killed her," Thad enunciated, patiently. "I didn't even see her until she was dead. Who else do you think - besides me - would do that to her?"

"I don't know," Timothy scratched his head.

"I want you to tell this to the police," said Thad. "Does Jill have any family? They couldn't trace anyone. Was Jill Johnson her real name?"

"Course it was," Timothy swore. "Police? You're crazy. Why would I talk to the police?"

"They need information."

"Not me," said Green. It was all they could get out of him after that. "Not me," he repeated. He began to doze. It was after three by now.

"I should take him home." Anne said.

"He can stay here - in my room," Thad said. "You too - you could sleep on the couch here."

"I don't think so, thanks. It's only a few blocks. Your flatmates don't seem very friendly."

"I'll come with you." He said. "You need help with him."

Between them they got Timothy down the stairs and walked through the quiet streets, hardly speaking. Even Timothy was quiet by now.

"That building on the left," said Anne after they walked through the dark streets about a quarter of a mile. "The basement flat. The door's in the back. Where's your key, Tim?"

He fumbled through his pockets and pulled out a key, then leaned against Thad. "Jill made a mess of things, didn't she?" he asked.

"Why do you say that?" Thad asked as Anne opened the door.

"They wouldn't kill her unless she messed it up, right?"

"I guess not," said Thad. "What exactly did she mess up?"

Timothy looked at him in the light of the hall as they went inside. "Oh, it's you," he said. "Shouldn't have said that to you, should I? Forget it."

"What's he talking about?" Thad asked Anne.

"I don't know. He says things like that sometimes. As if he thinks someone is going to kill him. Paranoid, Tim, that's what you are."

"I am not. Not me. Well, home sweet home. Come in. Have a drink."

Inside the small flat papers and magazines and clothing had been dropped wherever they were last used. Thad ended up walking on things that took him by surprise, like an old plate of half-eaten french fries which broke under his shoe. It was a tiny place with a living room and kitchen in the front, and a doorway at the back which he supposed led to bed and bathroom. Between them they got Timothy across the room and into a chair.

"This is his bed," Anne said, pointing out a mattress on the floor, covered with a loose knot of sheets and blankets. "He uses the other room as a darkroom."

"I can walk you home, if you like," said Thad.

"Thanks, but I'll stay here tonight. My flat is across the city. I hope that doesn't shock you. Tim said you were very conservative."

"I've been shocked before. Will you be alright here?"

"It's safer than walking home," she said.

"I could get you a cab." he said. She took his arm.

"Thad," she said. "Go home."

"Before you go, could you help me to the bathroom, old man?" Timothy called out. "I could use a wash before I take a doze." Then he leaned back, half snoring in the chair.

"Do you mind?" she asked.

"Not at all."

"But shut the door to the bathroom before you turn the light on. He's a fanatic about his darkroom staying dark."

"Of course. He always was a brilliant photographer, you know."

"He still is," she said.

A few minutes later, as Thad pulled Timothy out of the bathroom, Annie was straightening the sheets and blankets on the mattress. She had picked up the broken plate and put it into a trash container in the corner.

"You let him keep this garbage in the bathroom?" Thad put the glossy magazine on the cluttered table.

"What's it to you what he reads?" she asked. Her grey eyes were clear and level, and she still wore the heavy sweater over her sundress. "I think what Tim reads is Tim's business," she said. "If you hadn't looked at it, you never would have seen what it was."

"Well," he said, weariness coming over him suddenly like a blanket. "Goodnight."

"Goodnight. Let yourself out. The door will lock behind you." She turned her back on him. "Tim, honey, you've got to go to bed," she said. Thad went out and shut the door softly.

Heights

ða

When Peter Samuels, age four, woke up several hours later that same Sunday morning, he was in the crib where he had spent each night for the past two weeks. The shades were down and the room was still dark. He crawled out of the bed expertly and landed, softly, on the floor. Then he went to the door and pulled on the handle. Sometimes it opened and sometimes it didn't.

It opened. He padded, softly, down to the bathroom where he used the toilet and washed his face, just like Arulai had taught him. He would have brushed his teeth too, but there was no toothbrush. There was no sound around him in the house.

He was learning what to expect in this house, and when it was quiet like this in the morning, when he could open the door, it meant nobody was home. When nobody was home he didn't feel afraid, except sometimes at night. He went out into the hall in his pajamas and padded down the stairs to the rooms below. All the shades were down and the curtains were drawn. The front and back doors were locked. Peter didn't mind this. He was getting used to it. He liked being alone in the morning. It was the only thing he liked about his new house.

He padded into the kitchen and pulled open the refrigerator. There was milk there in small half-liter bottles he could handle by himself, and the cereal stayed on the kitchen table all the time. He liked cereal and milk and yogurt and crackers, but he was getting tired of them. He missed Arulai and his mommy very much. He wished he could find a telephone in the house, because he didn't think they knew he knew how to use it, but he did. Mommy taught him, right before they took him away from her. But if there was a telephone in the house, it never rang. And he couldn't find it. Some of the rooms were locked all the time.

He finished his cereal and put the dishes on the counter, then went into the living room and tried to look through the curtains. He did this every day in case he might see Arulai or his mommy. But there was nothing outside except bushes and trees. From the upstairs windows he could see the Alps far away and at night they glittered in moonlight with snow. But outside the house was nothing but trees and bushes and fields.

He put on his play clothes, in case Mommy would come and get him. They were the same clothes he wore when they grabbed him, out by the park, and pushed him into a big car, somebody's hand tight over his mouth. Maybe if he wore the same clothes, Mommy would know where he was. The lady had brought him new clothes, but he didn't like them.

He went downstairs again and turned on the television. There were no picture books in this house: just magazines and books he could not read. There were no games and no toys. He watched TV until he got hungry for lunch. By lunchtime maybe the lady would come. This was the lady who came every day, at different times. She brought his food and washed his dishes, and gave him a bath at night and put him to bed, reading him a story. But she usually drove away when he was in bed, and she always took the story with her. She wasn't a bad lady, he thought, but he did not like her because she wanted to be his new mommy. This did not make sense to him. Peter was not a stubborn child, but he knew she was not his mommy. And sometimes she brought a man with her. Peter didn't like him at all. He remembered him from the day when mommy was in the hospital and the babysitter let this man in to take pictures. Arulai ran out to the barn and hid until he went away, but Peter was too little. Peter didn't like this man. He didn't like the babysitter, either, after that.

He missed Uncle Jules' piggyback rides. He padded to the windows again, and then back to the TV. He stared at the television, listening for the car he knew would come, which he didn't want, and hoping his mommy would come instead.

There was a TV show that morning about some children who were bad and played soccer in the front yard of their house. They broke a window, and their mother was very unhappy, and the dog got out. But the dog hurt itself on the broken glass and they had to clean it with a towel. It was a towel that was specially treated so all the blood came out after one wash.

"I could break a window," thought Peter. "Then I could find someone who would take me to my mommy." He padded up to the bathroom and took his towel off the rack, then went downstairs again to look for a good window to break, a window he could climb through. He chose the low window in the kitchen, near the woods. He held the towel over his head, peaking through a fold in it as he hit the window hard with a big wooden spoon. When this didn't work, he threw a big metal spoon at it until it broke. It made a loud noise. Then, using his feet, he knocked out enough glass to climb out. Even with the towel he got hurt, but when he landed on the grass he didn't mind at all. He wiped his cuts with the towel and then dropped it in the grass and ran out toward the path along the road.

Peter didn't realize that this kitchen window was the first thing anyone would see as they arrived at the end of the long driveway. It was the first thing Linnet saw a half hour later, when she drove up into the yard with Stephen beside her. The bloodied white towel stretched like a flag beneath the broken window where Peter wiped his cuts.

"Something happened!" Linnet braked quickly and ran out. She hurried inside the house, her black low-heeled sandals crunching on the broken glass just inside the door. The empty cereal bowl was on the counter. The television was on, turned up loud. There was no sign of the little boy she had gone to so much trouble to get.

"He can't be far," she said coming back to the car. "We'll find him." Stephen was now in the driver's seat and Linnet ran around to the passenger's side. "Hurry!" she said. "He must have broken the window by himself. The little bastard. But I have his passport, and everything else is ready. We can wash him off on the way to the airport. Start the car, Stephen. We'll find him along the road, probably. I can prove he's my son to anybody we meet. We've got to search for him. Why are you just sitting there?"

Stephen turned to her, his hand resting calmly on the steering wheel. He held the car keys in his fingers.

"You're crazy," he said. "You're absolutely crazy."

"He's mine." she answered. "Everything is all ready. We have to make that flight."

"Do it yourself." he said, unmoving.

"I can't. You're sitting in the driver's seat with the keys, darling, in case you hadn't noticed. Move over."

Stephen looked far out into the fields of bright poppy and ripening wheat that stretched to the fringe of trees far in the distance. Behind them the ever-present shadow of the Alps rose on the other side of the unseen lake. His sunbleached hair was streaked with white against his leathered skin. His pale blue eyes reflected the blue sky. The sky seemed to go right through them.

"Listen, Linnet," he said, as he squinted at the horizon, his hand on the keys, and the wheel. "I am not risking any more for this child. Let him go. You've lost him now. Face it. Let him go back to his mother. Let him be found. If you go out now to look for him, a lost four-year-old with blood on his clothes from cut glass, people are going to notice, and they are going to ask questions. They are going to look at you and remember exactly what story you are telling them. It won't work. I tell you, it will not work. Do you understand?" He turned and transfixed her in his icy gaze. She tried to interrupt, but he took her by the shoulders. "No, listen to me. I can get you a dozen lads who will match that face on his passport. I can do it-" he looked at his watch - "right now if you like. You could make your flight and find him waiting for you at the next stop. Some small boy whose parents will not care. But not this one. You are not going to get me into trouble just for this one child. He still doesn't know our names. We can make sure he never sees us again. Let it go. It is too much of a risk."

"No," she cried. "This one is mine. He owes me a son. He wouldn't give me one. I'll take the only one he's got left to give me. You don't understand."

"I understand that you've gone crazy," he said. "Now you don't make any sense at all."

"Who are you to call me crazy?" She turned on him suddenly. "You constantly trade in children, but I don't think you have any feeling for them at all. I've done what I need to do for you. I can be as hardened about it as anyone. Ask Jasvinder in Banaras. He spent almost two years working with me. He's one of your best men. He'll tell you I can keep your secrets. All

I want, Stephen, is one child of my own, one child of *my* choosing - and you call me crazy? One child I can raise and be proud of, one child who won't get hurt, who you can't touch. This was the only way. I can't have any children, Stephen - don't you remember? You owe it to me."

"I owe you nothing, woman. Stop crying - it's ruining your face. As I recall, you got into trouble all by yourself."

"But Peter Samuels - Stephen, you said he would be no problem. I thought you understood - And now you want me to drop him, as if he was a dress I have to return to the store?"

"Calm down. That's not the point."

"And what is the point?"

"Now he's a problem is the point. I don't take risks like this," Stephen pointed to the window and the towel.

"You don't put sleeping children into empty houses? So what was last night all about - weight lifting?"

"Shut up. It's bad enough right now."

"So a little more trouble won't hurt."

"Not this kind of trouble. Not this child."

"I don't understand."

"Listen," Stephen said. "Wipe your nose on this. Stop behaving like a spoiled child and listen to me. It would be one thing if you found him, and he hasn't seen anyone, if he's still alone in the road or the woods. But someone is going to see you looking for him. He's probably met someone by now. Whenever you have to explain anything in this country, someone brings in the police. You do not want that, Linnet. I assure you, you do not want that."

"But I have his passport," she cried.

"So does his mother," Stephen shook her. "Don't you understand? If there is any questioning - especially right now -

about him being your son, the chances are very good that you will find yourself arrested for kidnapping. You will never have him that way."

"And I'll drag you down with me if you try and stop me," she said, pushing against him with his wet handkerchief. "I would rather die than live without that little boy, after all I've done to get him."

"Well, then, you just may," he said. They stared at one another. Then Stephen pushed her toward the open door. "Go on, then," he said. "Don't let me stop you. Go find him."

Linnet got out of the car. She straightened her sweater and smoothed out her hair slowly, deliberately. She wiped her face.

"It's Sunday," she said quietly. "People don't work here on Sunday mornings. I'm sure he hasn't seen anyone at all yet. It'll be alright." Stephen didn't answer. He watched her until she turned away and began to run down the road, out into the lane. Her voice called out, calling Peter's name.

Stephen put the car into reverse and backed slowly out of the driveway after her.

*

Katrien was not sure why she got Arulai up so early that same Sunday morning and dressed them both to go to church. It was a sudden impulse. She hadn't been to church in years, not since Peter was baptized in Delhi. That was Arul's idea. Before that, she went to church during the first year she was married. She and Arul came on Sundays to this very stone church in the center of Geneva where she first met Joanne Strecker.

She left Christina with Mrs. Roberts and they took the bus down to the plaza and crossed it to step over the stone threshold, up into the dark, wooden and stone church. Arulai held her hand. Men in suits greeted them quietly and gave them each a folded program.

"Thank you," Arulai said, looking around at the sanctuary with big eyes, still gripping her mother's hand. It was quiet, with more silver on the altar than she remembered, the light faintly coloured from the small, stained glass windows. The sanctuary was crowded with people in their good clothes, suits and hats. The organ started just as they were ushered into a seat halfway up the aisle. A fan in a corner circulated the smell of expensive perfume, incense and summer flowers.

"Look, Mama," Arulai whispered. "There's Georges!"

He sat with another man in the front of the church, dressed in a long white robe. Arulai stared at him. He saw them, and smiled. Shyly, the girl smiled back.

The service was familiar to Katrien, and she spent it gripping Arulai's shoulder, and sharing the books with her. She barely spoke, but looked down at the words and pointed them out. Arulai said them carefully, deliberately. It was not until they stood to recite the tenth psalm that Katrien began to listen to anything at all beyond the pounding in her chest.

> O Lord, why do you stand far off?
> Why do you hide yourself in times of trouble?
> ... In the pride of their countenance
> the wicked say "God will not seek it out...'
> Their mouths are filled with oppression
> ...They sit in ambush in the villages;
> In hiding places they murder the innocent.
> Their eyes stealthily watch for the helpless...

And the helpless fall by their might.
They think in their heart, 'God has forgotten,
He has hidden his face. He will never see it.'
...But you do see! Indeed, you note trouble
and grief, that you may take it into your hands...
Break the arm of the wicked and evil doers,
Seek out their wickedness until you find none...
Oh Lord, you will do justice for the orphan
and the oppressed,
So that those from earth may strike terror no more.

"Amen," said Katrien when it ended; she looked down at Arulai. "Amen," she whispered into the scented air. She was hardly aware of the service after that. She kept the prayerbook open to the psalm and found herself repeating the words over and over

Georges greeted them warmly when it was all over.

"Why do you wear a dress, Georges?" Arulai asked, taking his narrow stole in her hands and looking at the gold threads.

"Blame it on an emperor named Constantine," he answered. "I'm afraid it's all his fault."

"Georges, do you think I could speak with you?" Katrien asked. "In private? Is that possible?"

"Of course," he said, "Perhaps we could have lunch."

"I meant, without Arulai." She looked over to where the girl was carefully spelling out a poster on the entry wall.

"I see," Georges said, looking at her more carefully. "Perhaps when I am through here - it will be another hour or two - I could come and get you and we could go for lunch - without Arulai."

"Fine," she said. "As long as we don't go to Nefertiti's. Something more private, if you don't mind."

"Is something wrong?" he asked. "Is there any news about Peter?"

"No, nothing new is wrong." she said.

He rang her doorbell in the middle of the afternoon and they went down the rue Maunoir together to the lake and the park at the foot of the hill. They wandered through it, up to the Jet d'Eau, the stream of water which shot perpetually into the sky at this end of the lake, characterizing thousands of tourist postcards of Geneva, and cooling the air all around it. Georges led her to a small outdoor cafe and went inside to have a word with the cook, and to bring them a carafe of wine. The food, when it came, was surprisingly good and satisfying. Katrien could not remember the last time she had been fed so well.

"I know the chef," Georges said. "We share a love of good food, he and I - as you can probably tell." He put his palm over his belly.

"This wasn't what I had in mind," she said. "I wasn't asking for an invitation to lunch."

"No, I was the one who asked for that," he said. "You wanted a private talk. This is a good place for both. Because of the water, sound doesn't carry very well. In fact, it is probably more private than my office. Forgive me if I chose not to wear my priest's collar to lunch. You can still talk to me as a priest."

"You looked rather impressive in Constantine's dress." she said.

He smiled. "How long has it been since you were in a church?"

"A long time. A very long time. I went at school. Arul - my husband - and I met in your church - through Jules and Joanne Strecker."

"I see the Streckers now and then," he said.

"They called church friends to help me find our apartment,"
she said. "But I didn't expect to see you this morning. I need
a priest's advice, Georges. The psalm you recited - It moved me.
It was as if someone gave me words I had been looking for. I
wanted to use them to pray. I wanted to say those things. But
do you think it is right to pray if you don't believe?"

"I don't think I've met anyone who didn't believe anything, but
who still wanted to pray," he said. "What is it you don't
believe?"

"Oh, there are lots of things I don't believe," she said. "It's a
long story. You don't need my long story."

"But you feel that you need to pray?"

"Well, I have prayed sometimes. And things happen. It
scares me, because I don't believe in that kind of a God."

"You're afraid God may exist, even if you don't believe?"

"I don't know what I believe. But I want to pray. Is that
wrong?"

"No," said Georges. "God is not cruel. You should always
feel free to pray without being afraid of what might happen."

"Cruel. That's an interesting to word to use."

"Why?"

"Because - well, for a long time I was certain that God *was*
cruel. I thought only religious people and their god were cruel.
Until I was about twelve or thirteen, it was only the religious
people who were cruel to me. Everyone else was very kind.
Then - it changed. And I thought - after it changed - that maybe
it wasn't God's fault, after all."

"But you still don't trust God?"

"No, I don't. If there is a God. But - I prayed, and things
happened. Only once or twice, but it was too strange to be a
coincidence."

"Do you want to talk about it?" he asked.

She looked at him and remembered the party her stepfather took her to, the pools of water, and, long before that, the night she burned her hand on a light bulb when she was eight years old and prayed that she could tell someone what they were doing to her.

"No," she said. "I don't."

"Was your husband cruel to you?" Georges asked.

"Arul? Never. Not at all. Why would you think that?"

"You know," he said, "He wrote his name in the front of that Greek New Testament you lent me from your chalet. You said you met him in the church. Some might conclude from these things that he was a religious man."

"Yes," she said. "He was. I keep meeting religious men, for some reason. My father was an American preacher, you know."

"Ah."

"Yes. You'd think that would explain everything. My mother divorced him when I was ten or eleven. I came here with her. It was after that when I learned that other people could be evil, too. The church doesn't have a monopoly on the devil."

"That is true," said Georges calmly. They ate in silence for a few minutes. "So why today, after all these years?" he asked.

"You know, I don't know," she said. "I just woke up and - wanted to. Did you choose that psalm? It reminded me so much of Peter."

"And yourself?" he asked softly. "No, they're all determined for us," he went on so she could not answer. "I can choose the hymns and preach on what I like, but the readings have been fixed for a long time. There's a certain comfort, I find, in the repetition, in not having to start worship from scratch. You can worry and pray more effectively about immediate issues."

"You know," she said. "We owe you a great deal, the children and I. I realized all of a sudden that I hardly know anything about you at all. You've been very kind to us and I'm afraid I have taken you for granted. When we were up in the Jura, in the chalet, and I was talking about staying there, I suddenly realized how much we have depended on you since we moved in. It doesn't seem right."

"It is a pleasure to help," he said. "And some things were by accident - the photo, for example. That was certainly a mistake. If it had not come to me, I would hardly have an idea of what you have had to face the last few weeks. I don't think you would have told us very much."

"No. You're right. And if you weren't a priest, I probably would not have felt so free to ask you for help. Did you always want to be a priest?"

"No, I used to think I would go into business, like my father. He worked in wholesale clothing. Very secure, but it wasn't very exciting."

"Here?"

"No, in England. Like you, I had to choose my nationality."

"So you went to school in England?"

"And here. And you?"

"America. And here."

"That reminds me," he said. "Did I tell you I knew this fellow who knew you in India, Thad Hoskins?"

"Yes. You told me," she said.

"Oh, - yes, that day in the garden. I'm sorry."

"I don't like him, to tell you the truth. He was a bit too blundering and rude, insensitive."

"I thought perhaps you didn't like him. I'm sorry to remind you about him now."

"I was afraid you were going to try to match me up with him when you mentioned him to me the first time," she said.

"Match you up with him? Why would I do that?"

"You're a clergyman," she answered. "Most clergymen are uncomfortable about women with children who don't have a husband."

"I see," he said. "Let me assure you, Katrien, I would never try to match you up with Thad - or anybody else, in fact."

She frowned at him, and smiled. "Is that so?"

"Indeed," he said, smiling back.

"Well, that's very kind of you. No - " she raised her hand when he tried to speak again. "I think I know what you're saying, Georges. Is that why you wanted lunch, instead of a private interview in a church office?"

"Is that such a terrible thing?"

"No, of course not. I'm just surprised that you - that you would be interested in me. That's all. I'm not very sympathetic to religious things."

"But the psalm moved you," he said. "Why wouldn't I be interested in you? I've seen rather a lot of you. For me, that is."

"Well," she looked down into the wine, "Perhaps I'm thinking of the episode with Arulai about fathers. That was a bit awkward."

"And perhaps I'm thinking of all the occasions I have seen you being a good mother," he replied. "That has not been so awkward."

"But, what Arulai said is true. How do you know I'm not still involved with Christina's father?"

Georges looked out at the water, and then down into his glass. "I don't," he said at last. "It is true that I don't. But I have a high respect for marriage, you know, Katrien. And since you have never so much as mentioned Christina's father before this, and it seems probable that you are not married to him, I feel there is no sin for me to let you know of my interest. Perhaps I am wrong. Forgive me if I am."

"No," she said. "You're right. I've never heard anyone put it quite like that, certainly not a clergyman. They are usually more interested in condemning. You haven't even wondered about Christina."

"That is your business," he said. "If, as you say, you do not believe, then I think you need to live very consistently by your own values. They may be different from mine. I have no right to judge you, if you have a different system for your life, as long as you are honestly seeking in good conscience to live by it consistently."

"You're not like anyone I've ever met," she said. "And who can live consistently by their own values? I certainly can't."

"Neither can I," he said. "But I am still accountable to God for myself - and you for yourself."

"Not just myself," she said. "My children too. Do you ever think they will find Peter?"

"It is possible. It's not your fault."

"That's easy for you to say," she said. "But thank you, whether it's true or not." She stared out at the water on the lake, fingering the base of her wine glass.

"Katrien, are you - " he said slowly, after a long time, "Are you still involved with Christina's father?"

She looked over at him, at his shy, hesitant expression. He would die for my children, she thought. There's more to him than you realize at first. And he is really not unattractive; just a little paunchy and unassuming. A bit like a teddy bear.

"To be honest," she said, "I don't know."

Depths

❧

Timothy woke up that Sunday afternoon, as he usually did after he had too much to drink, thirsty for just a wee tiny bit more, just enough to calm his shattered nerves. Anne was prepared for this.

"It's in your coffee," she said. "Just that wee tiny bit and nothing more. I want you sober today."

"Damn what you want," he got up and staggered through the darkroom to wash and shave. He drank the coffee and ate the late lunch she had ready for him.

"Something tells me I made a blasted fool of myself last night," he said.

"You threatened Thad, blaming him for killing your old fiancée."

"Ooh, love, do you have to remind me so early?" he said. There was a sudden banging on the door. Timothy held his head. "Would you mind?" he cried. "Tell them to knock a little softer."

Anne went out to the hall. She had used the morning to take a long bath and change her clothes, and her appearance was a marked contrast to Timothy's.

She was back quickly, two men in uniforms at her shoulder.

"It's the police," she said helplessly. "They're here to search the flat. They have a warrant and everything."

The officers came in and showed Timothy their badges and the warrant. A third policeman came in behind them, all in uniforms and hats.

Timothy stood up, startled, but he still felt a little sick. He turned grey and sat down again.

"Go ahead," he said, gesturing to the chaos around him. "You're not going to find anything here but a lot of dirty pictures. It's my specialty. No law against it."

"We'll see about that," one man said.

"What do you mean, 'not anything but dirty pictures?' asked another. "What else do you think we expect to find?"

"If you want to search, man, search," said Timothy. "Don't waste your time criticizing my grammar for God's sake."

They searched for most of the remaining afternoon, most of it in the darkroom. They did, as he said, find a large quantity of the sort of photos he had predicted, and he was surprised when they managed to find several regulations against him. Anne stayed in the front room with him most of the time, cleaning up after the police had gone through everything there.

"Oh, so you do have a rug," she said.

"Shut up," he muttered. "I wonder why they show up today. I mean, they come very prepared, you notice."

"I asked them," she said. "They said it was a phone call."

"Damn prepared for a phone call."

"Do you think it was Thad?" she asked. "He went through to the bathroom last night."

Timothy swore at Thad in no uncertain terms.

"Who else could it be?" Anne asked.

"Shut up. They're standing right there."

"Well, I don't have anything to hide!" she shouted. "How did I know you did?"

"Shut up, will you?"

Anne stopped talking. She sat down and started to look for something to read.

"Don't read that," Timothy said. "That's my old college copy of *Ulysses*. They might arrest you for reading it."

"I've read it before," she said, putting it down.

"So read it again. You might learn something new."

"It's not a dirty book," she said. "Not unless you have a dirty mind."

"That's news to me," he answered, staring into space as the sound of papers and drawers opening and shutting echoed in the background. "What else did I tell Thad last night?" he asked.

"How should I know? You want to phone him and ask?"

"Expect I'm not supposed to make phone calls at the moment," he said. "Try to remember what else I said."

"No," she said. "If you don't remember, it's your own fault."

"Not my fault somebody killed my fiancée. You'd get drunk, too, if somebody told you that all of a sudden. Shot her through the head, he said. I remember that much."

"So why didn't you ever tell me about her?" Anne demanded.

"Why dig up the past?" he answered. "Jill was in the past. Fat. Jolly, Pushy. Sneaky. Definitely in the past."

"You don't sound very unhappy that she's dead."

"What do you know? I wasn't unhappy that she was in the past. But I'm very unhappy that she is dead. She owed me a bit of money, she did."

"Oh, I see. Well, I'm glad I haven't borrowed any money from you."

"Haven't got any to lend."

"Then how did you get it to lend it to her?"

"I didn't lend it to her. She stole my whole bloody bank account, can you believe it, and went off with it to India. Every blasted centime."

"Along with the letter you forged for her for Thad?"

"Shut up. They'll hear you."

"I think they have heard me. And I heard you last night admitting it to him. You also admitted forging a cheque."

"What kind of woman are you, witnessing against me?"

"Don't start insulting me," she answered. "I think you're in enough trouble."

"Damn it, I think you're right," he said, looking around him at the policeman in the doorway. "Excuse me," he said. "Who's in charge here?"

The policeman in charge came out from the darkroom.

"If I wanted to make a statement," said Timothy, "A very long statement, every bloody word of it true, implicating a whole lot of other nasty people, just like me, some of them worse if you can believe it, could I do it here, or would I need to go down to police headquarters?"

"If you want to make a taped statement, we could take you down to headquarters."

"Well then, let's go," said Timothy. "What are we waiting for? If I'm going to get into so much trouble for this little bit of nothing here - " he gestured toward the other room, "Then, damn it, I'm going to bring the whole house down for you."

"Come with me then," said the policeman.

▪

Peter hurried through the underbrush. He had met a dog and some birds and a rabbit, and even a whole field full of spotted cows, but nobody he could yet actually ask to take him home to his mommy. He did not yet know how to tie his shoelaces and he kept tripping over them. He had never walked so far all alone. He could see houses in the distance, but they never seemed to get any closer. He followed the road, hiding from it now and then when a car went by, afraid it would be the lady coming back to the house. It was a bright day and the sun made him hot and a little bit dizzy. Beyond the field of cows he saw more trees beside the roadway. He would get cool once he was inside the trees again.

As he approached the woods, he saw an old lady in rubber boots. She was walking across the road and toward the field on the other side, a bucket in her hand.

"Madame!" he called. "Madame! Madame!" It was what everyone called ladies here, though he did not know very much French yet. He had not spoken in a day or two and his voice came out hoarse and soft. She didn't hear him. "Madame!" he called, more loudly. Then, just as he thought the woman saw him, he heard a pounding behind him and turned to see Linnet running toward him across the field. He ran as fast as he could toward the road, toward the village woman who now definitely saw him. But she was farther away than he thought, and he tripped over his shoelaces just as he reached the road. He felt Linnet's shadow over him and the grip of her hands reaching down to lift him off the ground and, in the distance, the sound of the car he knew so well coming toward them on the road.

❧

Willi spent most of Sunday morning in police headquarters, poring over the English transliteration of the lists and memos with the rest of the team. It was an international team, specially formed for this case, and only a small part of it was there in the office with him, scribbling down names and addresses, checking them against computer files, and making phone calls. The rest were gathering themselves into place in several different cities in Europe and India, waiting for further information. The goal was not simply to stop the operation by identifying those involved in the sale of these children. There were also a large number of children who might be found and returned to their parents. Willi had also called for, and reviewed, the file on Peter Samuels. His name was nowhere on the lists. They were also looking for any possible connection between Linnet and the man she was staying with, Stephen Whitby. So far this too had turned up nothing. In addition, they were searching for the girl who brought the papers into Strecker Translators, but she was apparently away for the weekend. Willi spent most of the afternoon entering names into the computer and looking for all possible links with India. He was beginning to feel that his coworkers considered this a minor problem compared to the loss of so many European children and as he continued to draw blanks he grew more and more intolerant of this.

Finally, in a moment of complete frustration, he checked the computer for Katrien herself. Switzerland took great care about who it let in, and who stayed. He was surprised to find she was a Swiss citizen. Why had he thought she must be an American? Well, her father was American. He was surprised again when he learned she owned a chalet in the Jura, previously in her mother's name. He traced her mother, and then her stepfather, and stopped. Her stepfather, Maurice Whitby, was currently in prison for a long history of theft and embezzlement. His oldest charges on record, however, were for - child molesting and indecent exposure. Willi probed the file further and calculated the dates. Katrien would have been away, in private school, during these years. He wondered how safe she had been. And what had her stepfather done for a living? Willi searched through a few more files and then stopped. Maurice Whitby had been a partner in an art reproductions business with one Stephen Whitby, his brother.

It wasn't much, but it was enough to follow-up Stephen. Whitby owned a number of businesses in Geneva, and several in bordering cities. Willi made a few phone calls. Just then the police brought in Timothy and Willi was permitted to be present to hear Timothy's statement. Timothy liked an audience, and he spared no details.

Anne came into the station with him, but stayed in the waiting room. She asked the attendant for something to read, and was reading a French paper when they took Timothy out and charged him. She asked if they wanted her for anything. They took her name and address and told her to go home. She left the paper at the desk and went out to catch a bus.

As she came out of the station, she saw Thad, coming across the street. "Is Green here?" he asked, as they met outside the heavy gates. "I called the flat and someone said he was talking to the police."

"They just charged him, thanks to you," she said.

"Me? What did I do?"

"You called the police, didn't you, last night, after you looked in his darkroom?"

He frowned at her, puzzled. "I don't know what you're talking about," he said. "You mean his darkroom was worse than his bathroom?"

"You didn't call the police?"

"No. I went home and went to bed. Why would I call the police?"

"I won't begin to tell you," she said. "They won't let you see him now. He's in for a long time. Have you had dinner?"

"No," he looked at his watch. "I'm supposed to give a talk in a church in an hour and a half. Would you like to come along?"

"How fun," said Anne, "Why not?"

*

A little over an hour later Willi finally left the station and got into his car to drive, alone, across town and out into the Jura. He had only gone a few blocks when a call came on the car phone.

"Hello, Samuels here."

"Yes. Sergeant Ballein. You asked me about the plane reservations which the woman, Linnet, made for today?"

"Yes?"

"You're right. She was planning to travel with a child. She asked about a children's menu. But she missed the flight."

"You're sure?"

"Absolutely."

"Did you check other flights?"

"Yes. Nothing. We don't know the child's name, of course, but we suspect she had a false passport ready. We're guessing it was an English passport, since that's what she carries."

"The flight was for Heathrow?"

"Gatwick. Special arrangements. Lots of private options from there, if your papers are in order."

"But they missed it."

"Yes."

"That's not good."

"No."

"Any more information from Timothy Green's statement?"

"You heard it all. Oh, he knows the girl who brought in those papers. Photographed her now and then. No idea about the papers, he says."

"Should we believe him?"

"Hard to tell. He probably didn't need to write down names and addresses. He seemed to remember details very well. Photographic memory, he said he had," the sergeant noted, dryly.

"I could use one right now," said Willi. "I seem to be lost, all of a sudden. Could you check a map and tell me where I'm supposed to be going?" He listened and made notes on the pad in front of him. Cars honked at him. The light had turned. "Thanks," he said.

Before long he pulled up into the drive of Katrien's cottage. The police knew he was coming here, but he hadn't expected to find several police cars ahead of him in the lane. He hadn't expected anyone at all.

"What's this?" he asked the man at the gate, as he got out. "Have you found something?" The policeman looked up at him.

"Can I see your identification, sir?" he said. Willi never wore a uniform, and as a result always had to show his papers, sometimes including his passport, to new officers here. Until they knew who he was, they often squinted at him as if he was a suspect. The curse of the foreigner, he thought. The curse of being a dark-skinned man in such a white country. Even the sky here was white half the time. How could Arul accept a fellowship to study here? Willi fit in among the Egyptian and Iranian and Lebanese foreigners in Geneva, people with whom he had nothing in common but his complexion. Among his coworkers he was a complete stranger. If international relations are this awkward for the police, he thought, why do they work so effectively among the criminals of the world?

He pushed through the door and into the chalet. A policewoman stood in the kitchen, the same policewoman, if he had known it, who wanted to question Arulai, but was not allowed. She recognized him.

"What happened?" he asked her.

"A call came an hour ago," she said. "One of the neighbors was trying to get through to the police all morning. She knew the house was empty so she got suspicious when a van arrived in the middle of the night. She thought they were loading up furniture. In reality, they were unloading children."

Willi looked around. It was true. The living room was full of children, lying in chairs, on the couch, on the floor, all between three and ten years old, he guessed, and all absolutely silent.

"Are they dead?"

"No, thank God. But they have been drugged to keep them quiet. There are more in the bedroom. The doctor is with them. Some may have been overdosed. They think someone who was about to drive them across the border suddenly panicked, and dumped them here."

"You say there was a van?"

"They pushed it down the hill. The plates are missing. They're examining it now.

"Why would someone bring them here?"

"I would like to know that myself," she said. "The woman who owns this - "

"Yes, I know. Her son disappeared a few weeks ago. Is he here?"

"No."

"You're sure?"

"I interviewed his mother. I had his picture," she said. "All three of her children had an Indian father. There are no foreign children here. These are all Swiss children."

"Three? She only had two children. I know - she was my brother's wife."

"Well, your brother's wife has a three month old baby girl who looks just like her brother and sister. Don't look so surprised. It happens in every family now and then. At any rate, the boy's not here."

"I see," Willi said, looking around at the mass of pale, drugged children. He took off his glasses and wiped his face with his handkerchief. "Where's the telephone?" he asked. She pointed him to the hallway. "Do they know where these children were before they came here?"

"Not yet. We're hoping the children will be able to tell us."

The phone rang. An officer put his head in the room.

"News," he said. "The driver of the van was picked up early this morning outside the house by a car whose plate number we have - registered under one -" he looked down. "Stephen Whitby. A woman was driving. Thank heavens for over-inquisitive neighbors."

"Now we have him," said Willi.

"Message for you, too, Samuels. They called from Whitby's studio downtown. Said there is a lot there relevant to your investigation."

"The Samuels boy?"

"No, he's still missing. Papers and photos, I believe. More of this English-Urdu code, too, they say. Here's the address."

"Tell them I'll be there as soon as I can."

"Right."

&a

Stephen Whitby drove a long way north that afternoon. He switched the plates on the car with those from the stolen van, then took the mountain roads up through the Jura, careful not to cross the border into France. He stopped in a small village to make several long distance phone calls, then drove off again. Linnet and the boy slept soundly in the back seat.

Stephen was puzzled. He didn't know what to do with them now. He was no killer. He never killed anyone in his life. To think about killing them made him sick. But he had enough morphine to keep them asleep as long as necessary, and he knew how to use it. He wouldn't kill them with it, not even by accident. And why should he kill them? But what else could he do with them? Linnet was the killer. She had even admitted it to him. Could he force her to kill herself? That was an idea. No, that would make him sick, too. And the boy - why did they have to get him involved at all? They could trace Whitby to Katrien too easily. He didn't want that. He had run his business anonymously for years. This was not the time to be traced. Why did Linnet have to choose this particular child, out of all the children Stephen could have given her? Usually he let her have what she wanted. He let her go to India whenever she wanted. Let her sleep with his friends. He wasn't the jealous type. He was generous. She was loyal. She kept his secrets and spent her own money. They were good for each other. But she never wanted a child before. She never threatened him before. No one threatened Stephen Whitby. No one.

He wanted to be left alone, really. He was a wealthy man, after all. He gave unwanted children the chance for a good life, didn't he? Picked them out of their pitiful surroundings in the villages and gave them a chance for some of the good things in life. How many street children got the opportunity to work with professional photographers like Green, like himself? They had good bodies, those kids. He gave them a real chance in life, didn't he? They never died while they were in his care, did they? Once they left it, well, that was not his business. But he was not like some of these people who deal in children for their own perverted pleasures. Maurice, for example. He was a real bastard. Well, he got into trouble on his own. Stephen didn't have anything to do with that. Besides, there was no money in it. No glamour. No moment of glory in the darkroom when you looked down at the shadows in your hand and saw that you had a real winner.

Stephen drove fast, a bit too fast, through the mountains, thinking of the mountains in Kentucky when he first drove out to rescue Katrien from her father's denigrating pit of filth and poverty. He would never forget the small, pale scrawny child he first saw crouching like an animal on the splintered steps. Her cavernous, brilliant eyes looked up, startled at the rented blue Jaguar, looked up directly into his eyes, as if she could see right through his dark glasses. Something red had spilt down her legs onto the dark boards of that shack they called a church, spilt in big, running drops, like fresh menstrual blood, the blood of a young virgin, the blood of the damned. Stephen's blood. He shook himself. Her mother paid Stephen well to fly to Kentucky and rescue the girl. And she had some real potential. Why did he ever let his brother get involved with her mother? It changed everything. He had to rescue her again, once or twice, for no money at all. Maurice would have ruined her at that party in Geneva, so she'd never be good for anyone after that, if Stephen hadn't been there with his camera that night. He did what he could for her. It was only right. But the whole operation was a waste. He swore never again to answer these cries for help, to restore a child to its parents, no matter how much money he could make from it. He had certain principles, after all. Parents, for the most part, were evil. The people they married were even worse. Better to give the child a chance with other people, a chance to grow up free of the shame of your genes. He wished he could have left Katrien out of all this. Would she never stop following him now? He would wake up in the night in a cold sweat, seeing again those skinny knees and solemn eyes staring down at him from the dark plank steps in that east Kentucky parking lot, in the very pit of hell. All for a nice bundle of money he spent rather quickly. He wished he had never seen Katrien. Why did Linnet want this particular boy? He didn't understand it at all.

He enjoyed the pull of the car as he raced through the mountains. He knew it would only last a little while longer. It was all over now. Claire Feuillet stole his papers and now messages were coming in that the police knew a little too much. True, Stephen had been just a bit harsh with Claire when he found out, even when she swore she told them she found the papers in her father's desk. She had been getting too greedy lately. But it didn't matter. Her father's reputation was as clean as the top of Mont Blanc. Sooner or later, they would trace it back to Stephen Whitby.

At midnight he checked his charges, covered them gently with a blanket against the night air, and turned the car back toward Geneva. He smiled, and turned on the radio. How long would it take them to decipher the Urdu script? No one would suspect him of that. He was the proverbial playboy. When did he have time to learn Urdu? No one would guess. No one.

Even his service record, which said he had spent three years as an international volunteer trying to maintain peace along the Pakistani border after Independence, said nothing about him learning to read and write several languages. He learned that in the villages. That was his secret.

He drove calmly through the night, stopping once for gas, then turning to thread the car down through the hills into Lausanne just before dawn. If they were searching for him, they would expect him to cross the border, not return to Geneva. What was more innocent, after all, than driving home from a long weekend on a Monday morning with his girlfriend and her son asleep in the back of the car? He had all the passports, after all. He had destroyed the tickets.

He checked his watch. They would begin to wake soon. Let them, he thought. By the time they are fully conscious, we will be home again. It's too bad he had to bring the child into the flat. He had always been very strict about maintaining an 'adults only' flat, never even letting a child in. It didn't seem right, somehow. Well, there was a time for everything. A time for life. A time for death. He smiled to himself as the sun rose over the lake and the icy stillness of the Alps reflected in the clean, waxed hood of his car.

❧

As the sun rose over the city that Monday morning, Thad woke up, vaguely troubled. At first he couldn't remember why. Then he remembered. It was Anne. Why did it bother him so much? Why did women always bother him so much? Had she taken him seriously yesterday at all? He really didn't know. She was Green's girlfriend, after all. But she seemed to take everything so - well, so casually. He didn't understand it.

They had eaten dinner at a Chinese place near St. Peter's in the old city. Then they sat on the porch of the church and talked for a while. She told him what Green said about Jill Johnson, but he was still confused. Why would anyone go to India just to play a joke on him? Besides, he never liked jokes. He never quite *got* them. Eleven years ago, when he first volunteered with the mission, the year Arul Samuels was with them as a volunteer, Arul was always playing jokes on Thad. Everybody liked Arul, but then he turned out to be brilliant and left them all to go to graduate school. Thad didn't like Arul's jokes, because they made everybody laugh at him, but at least they were funny. At least, he thought, they were trying to make him laugh at himself. He never could quite bring himself to do this, but what Jill did - that was a very different thing. He felt a little bit like Anne, too, was laughing at him in the same way last night in the parish hall as he gave his talk on overseas missions. He used all the standard language. Words everybody understood. And she hadn't understood any of them.

"What's this about a commission?" she asked. "And God laying on your heart - really, that's a funny way to put it. And why do you talk so much about hidden people groups when you just mean subcultures? If you really want people to understand what you are saying, Thad, I think you need to speak English a little more clearly."

This bothered him. What was wrong with her, that she didn't understand? He tried to talk to her for a long time after that, but it didn't work very well. The harder he tried, the more she laughed at him. He invited her up for dessert and Jim gave her a synopsis of his sermon, but she kept laughing. Thad invited her, again, to stay on the couch if she had nowhere else to go, but she said she would get a cab instead and go home to her perfectly adequate flat.

"Your problem, Thad," she told him, rather late in the evening, "Is that you don't know how to act normal. Be yourself."

"I am myself," he said glumly. "And you tell me it's not normal."

"You were normal yesterday," she said. "When Tim and I came in here last night, you were completely normal. But today you put on some kind of 'holiness' hat. It doesn't work. Don't you feel all uptight, standing in front of a church talking in your funny language?"

"Not particularly," he said.

"Oh, you're hopeless," she said. "But you're a nice hopeless. Come to Tim's trial with me. They're going to throw the book at him, and I'd like to hold somebody's hand."

"Tim might not be very happy about that," he said.

"I don't think he will worry, if it's your hand," she said.

"Doesn't redemption mean anything at all to you?" he asked, desperately.

She smiled. "It's what I can't do to Tim," she answered. "It's illegal. Here's my cab. I must go. Be yourself, Thad. That's all you need to do." She kissed him on the lips and ran out to the cab in the lane.

He stared at the doorway for a long time, until Jim shouted to him that the bathroom was free if he wanted it. He looked at his watch. He had to be in the office by 8. How could he try and act normal on so little sleep? He was normal last night when Green came in accusing him of murder? He tried to remember how he had acted. All he could think of, instead, was Anne's kiss. It bothered him for a long time Sunday night, and when he woke on Monday morning he had to take aspirin because he had a headache from thinking about it.

He still had his headache when the police cars raced past him along the rue de Lausanne, on his way to work. He rubbed the back of his neck as the sirens went by.

Why should he go to Green's trial, he thought with a sudden rush of anger. He never wanted to see or hear about another policeman in his life. The light changed, just then, and he went up into the office, holding his neck against the encroaching headache.

And all creation

❧

Stephen Whitby was at home when the police found him a few minutes later. He opened the door himself, listened to the charges against him, and went with them quietly, like a child, like the hundreds of children he had taken, quietly, and destroyed. He said he felt sick to his stomach. That was all he said at first. They found Linnet and the boy leaning against the bed in the adjoining room. They had not been dead long, maybe an hour said the coroner. Stephen's fingerprints were still on the gun. He had put it down to answer the door. He was still trying to decide whether or not to shoot himself. But she was going to kill me, he told them in a soft, reasonable voice as they led him to the car. She was going to kill me, he repeated over and over as the police drove him quietly through the morning streets. How can I live without her now? Give the gun to the little boy, he said, and the little boy will kill myself. But the police, not being court psychiatrists, never wondered which little boy he meant. They knew something Whitby did not know they knew. Claire Feuillet, daughter of one of Geneva's most respected banking executives, was found dead in an overgrown corner in the garden of Katrien Samuel's chalet. She had been beaten to death some time in the previous 24 hours. The little boy killed me, Stephen said meekly when they finally opened the door and led him into the police station. Sure he did, they said. Sure he did.

*

Willi spent most of Sunday night and Monday morning with the police team in Stephen's studio, sorting through boxes of photos and papers. When he finished at the studio he viewed Whitby's apartment, briefly. From there he drove across the city to Katrien's.

"I saw you in the street on Saturday night," she said. She was alone. "I have a friend coming for us at 5," she said. "We'll stay with them for a few days. Did you see the body?"

"Which body?"

"How many bodies are there?"

Willi shook his head. "You saw Peter."

"I had to identify him." She spoke without emotion. "I didn't expect to ever see Peter again, but I never thought they would kill him."

They sat together on the couch in the midafternoon, a pot of fresh coffee between them. Willi's trousers were dusty from a long night with old papers and photographs. He had taken time to shave and change his shirt. Katrien's face was lined with shadows but she had dressed carefully. Since she saw him Saturday night, she knew he would come sooner or later.

"They think Whitby was desperate. He was crazy. Have you told Arulai?"

"She's in school. I - I just couldn't go and get her yet to tell her Peter is dead. Georges - the priest downstairs - will meet her."

"You know Peter was with Linnet - she took him, and they died together?"

"Yes," she sipped her coffee.

"Katrien, I'm sorry," he said.

"It's strange, Willi. I knew my own son for less than two years of his life. The first six months we were here I had them in therapy - well, all three of us. I didn't know what they might have gone through. Arulai did well, but Peter didn't like it. He had a man for a counselor. I wonder if that was right. It was really more a play group - but I still wonder."

"And how did it go for you?"

"Me? Oh," she looked up and smiled in a distracted way. "It was fine. My mother put me in therapy the first two years I was with her, when we came to Switzerland, when I was ten. Then it stopped. She married Maurice and I changed schools. Then she had a nervous breakdown - or a brain tumor - or something. They never told me what really happened. I think she just gave up coping. Sometimes it's enough to have good friends, friends who are capable of really feeling with you. Not always, but sometimes it's enough. I don't think my mother felt she had any friends she could trust. You know, I don't understand why you are here at all - or how you know so much about what happened."

"I'm a policeman."

"A policeman?"

"An investigator. Recently we have been investigating Indian children who disappear. But I work with the police department."

"Why didn't you ever tell us?"

"The nature of my work. It's better if people think I am just a government worker involved in paperwork. And, in this case," he paused.

"You suspected me of wanting to harm them? Is that why you were watching the flat?"

"I suspected you were involved in some way. I realized some time ago that I was misled. You knew?"

"You never liked me when we lived with you. You thought your parents were right when they took the children away. Do you still suspect me?"

"No. I've just come from Stephen's studio. We spent most of the night going through it. There are boxes, going back many years, of disturbing photographs, most of them of children. He tried to destroy them but didn't have the time. I was concerned chiefly with any evidence of Indian children, but I will have to go through most of his photos and papers for this information. He was not just selling photos and information; he was also selling children. I suspect you knew that. It will take days to sort out. It was not pleasant work."

"How does that vindicate me?"

He leaned against the arm of the couch and faced her across the thick, worn tapestry. "You knew for a long time that Linnet would try to take away your son. How did you know that?"

She shook her head and looked down into the coffee. "What do you mean?"

"Are you denying that Linnet had a strong hold on you for Peter? Wasn't it this pressure that kept you involved long after you must have wanted to forget everything?"

She looked up at him. "I just asked what you meant. As you say, none of this is a pretty story. How much do you already know?"

"When did Stephen take those photos of you? There are two or three dozen of them. How old were you?"

"Oh, god, this is awful," Katrien pushed her cup, clattering, onto the glass of the coffee table. "So now you've seen them. They're public property, now, aren't they?" She got up and began to pace across the room. "You know, Willi, I didn't care if he published them. The kind of audience he'd get - I wouldn't know anyone who looked at them, and they wouldn't know me - or wouldn't admit it. But then when he told me he could send them to people I knew - people like your parents - years after it - when I thought everything was all over."

"The pictures strengthen the charges against him, not against you. How old were you?"

"Do you really want to hear this?" she asked him from the window.

"I really want to see him and his associates locked up for a long time," he said. "But I don't want to force you. We know more than we once thought we wanted to know about each other. We are on the same side now, I think. Anything you can do to help them prosecute this man may save many children's lives. I saw the photos in the context of the man who took them, and his world. If you don't want to add anything to that, I will understand. But you may want to help us prosecute him."

She stared into space, then ran her hands through her hair, and began to pace.

"I'll tell you." she said. "It's his curse, not mine. Let him take it and carry it to hell with him." She stared out the window, fingering the lace panels. Cars passed in the street below. They listened to the urban silence for a long time before she began to speak.

"I was very young the first time." She didn't look at him as she spoke. She turned to pace again, stopping now and then by the windows, continuing to talk as she looked down into the street, never looking at him. "It was right before my mother married again. I didn't know why he was doing it. I thought I knew what abuse was - it didn't have anything to do with - sex.

161

Not that there was - it was just all very suggestive. Stephen was nice to me that first time. Nothing threatening. Just a game, you know. Can you believe there was actually a time when I liked Stephen? During the year after we came to Switzerland, he was very good to us. It's how they start out - try to get you more comfortable. Then he introduced my mother to Maurice, his brother. My mother wanted to marry again. She wanted to marry Stephen, but he wasn't interested. Maurice was. Stephen took the first pictures right before Maurice married my mother. One day about a year later my mother and I were talking about things she didn't understand about Maurice and I told her about Stephen and the pictures. Soon after that she found out he had a police record. Maurice I mean, not Stephen."

"For child molesting."

"You know? It was during his first marriage. My mother found out before he tried it on me. I think that's when she stopped coping. She had worked so hard to get me away from my father - now this. All my real father did was spank me routinely, forcefully constrain me in what the law considered an abusive manner, deprive me of my rights to an education and sometimes make me go hungry. Nothing really bad, you know? She sent me to boarding school in Zurich. She said it was for my education, to get me away from Stephen. I wish she told me the truth. Stephen never came to see us once after she married Maurice. She didn't need to try to get me away from Stephen."

"And the next time?"

"The other photos? You have seen everything now, haven't you," she said bitterly. Willi didn't answer. He watched her from the couch, unmoving, waiting. She had never seen him like this.

"I was seventeen," she went on. "That's when I found out about Maurice. My mother was in an institution by then - an expensive clinic. One weekend I went home and Maurice took me to a party. They shut me up in a room with them, Stephen and Maurice. Linnet was there."

"Linnet?"

"Yes. Stephen called her his business manager. Why?"

"Nothing. Go on."

"It was hell. Pure sadism. Maurice really tried to come at me, but Stephen wouldn't let him. Sounds like a kindness, doesn't it? It wasn't. Child molesters are shy, you know - they don't want to be seen. So Stephen and Linnet started taking pictures - wouldn't stop. They wouldn't let me alone. Everything kept flashing. I couldn't see anything. It was hard to believe it was really Stephen. He was a completely different person than I had known before. He just photographed me those two times. But the things they tell you to do... Well, you've seen them. Maurice never did touch me, all because Stephen insisted on making it into a grand form of art. Stephen seemed to think he was doing me some favor. Like I would die if he wasn't there to rescue me from the bastard's gross physical act with the bright lights of his little camera. Oh, it was art, alright. Do you know what it's like to feel like you're being visually raped for hours, with bright lights on, and people you hate all around you, and everyone getting close, everybody looking at you, masturbating with their eyes, if you'll excuse my language? Oh, it's an art form, I'll tell you. Abuse is their high and holy art. Sadism takes a lot of skill; Stephen taught me that. Stephen is not at all religious but it was almost as if he was that night. I mean, it wasn't like a ritual or anything. It's just that he was so sure he was right, that what he was doing was so beautiful, that nothing he did could possibly be wrong or hurt me. And meanwhile there he was violating everything there was about me. Violation of the body can scar a person for life. But it's the violation of the mind, of the emotions that can destroy you completely. After what they did to me, I felt it happen over and over again, exactly the same way, whenever I went out into the street, fully dressed, and a man looked at me. You wouldn't understand this. You think it is a compliment to look at a woman. But there is a very fine line - it's true about women, too. My stepmother used to look at my body like she owned it absolutely and could do whatever she liked. Once she tried, and I hit her. I might be dead, if my father hadn't come in. Not that he ever defended me, but at least he never looked at me like that. But after Maurice's party I couldn't bear it at all. To have men or women look at my body against my will - even fully dressed. For years it felt like I was being violated all over again any time anyone except Arul really looked at me. I think that is partly why I felt so safe in India, when I was married. At least it's culturally acceptable for women to hide in groups of women, to hide behind layers of clothing. When Arul died, I suddenly felt naked all over again. That's why you thought I went crazy with grief. It wasn't just grief for Arul. It was grief for myself. I was finally forced to face what they had done to me, and to come to terms with it. It almost destroyed me, Willi. And that's what they do to these children. They endure it for years. And I condemned my own son to that, because I believed them when they said they would leave me alone if I did, that everything would be normal again. I have to live with that."

"I think you have lived with it for long enough," he said. "I don't think it would have changed what happened to Peter. There were factors beyond your control. It was not your fault."

"I'm surprised to hear you say that."

"It's true."

"I know. Didn't I tell you I was in therapy all winter?"

"How did you meet Linnet?"

"I told you. She was at that party. You won't find any photos of her. She's a pillar of discretion. Was. Sorry. Then after Arul and I were in India, she found me again."

"Found you?"

"I went out shopping, it was my very first week in New Delhi and I met her on the way home. She got me into her apartment. Said she had something important from Geneva for me. I thought it must be something about my mother. Instead, she told me Stephen and she were going to send Arul's parents the photos they had of me - that it would force Arul to leave me - but if I agreed to give her my son, she would leave me alone and everything would be fine."

"Your son? Your first trip to India?"

"That's just it. Arulai was a baby. How did I know I would ever have a son? It's easy to give over something you don't have. I felt very differently once I had Peter. And - well, she has a way of persuading people. I wanted to see Arul again. I wanted to leave the house alive."

"It was just the two of you?"

"Yes. So why didn't I just walk out? I've asked myself that lately. When I was a child, it was my stepmother who thought up all the creative ways to punish me. My father let her do whatever she liked. My father was only bad when he had to preach, but it was always dangerous to resist Barbara. Always. And any resistance made it much worse. They thought that destroying a child's self-confidence was a holy act - breaking the will, they called it. For a while they succeeded in breaking mine.

They probably would have successfully destroyed me if they had me before I was five, if there was no way out. There was something about Linnet that caused me to react to her as I used to react to my stepmother. I was terrified to resist. I felt that she was much stronger than me."

"So you agreed."

"In the end. I never told Arul. I was always afraid he would find out. I should have told him. We could have stopped it. And why my son? I don't understand that. She traded in children all the time. Why did she need mine? She has him - now." She started to cry for the first time. He watched her. She stood by the window, staring out at the narrow lane, the brick sidewalk, the Arabic sign over Nefertiti's down the street, as they blurred in the afternoon sun. He stood up. She shook her head. "I'll be alright," she said. "I'm glad you came." She walked from the window and took a Kleenex from a box on the coffee table. It was a garish box, matching nothing in the room, nothing he knew of her. She saw him staring at it. "My landlady gave it to me," she said, smiling through her tears. "It's one of the ugliest things I've ever seen." She sat down in the small French chair beside him. He was silent as she stared at the Kleenex box. She was hardly aware now that she was crying.

"It is my guess," Willi began after a long time - "That Linnet would say that she wanted your son because I refused to give her any."

Katrien looked over startled, from her tears.

"You? What did you have to do with it?"

"Rather a lot, I'm afraid. She was my wife."

She stared at him. "Your wife? You mean - Arul said - He said you were married once, but I was never supposed to ask you about it. It was her?"

"Yes."

"I'm sorry," she said. "I had no idea. And now she's dead."

"Our marriage was a mistake," he said. "Our fathers wanted it. She was very beautiful, and I agreed. For a month - maybe less - I thought it was a good, traditional marriage. Then it became clear, that she was - whatever she was - "

"You caught her with Arul, didn't you?"

It was true. She knew by his face.

"Don't be foolish," he said. "Why would you think such a thing?"

"She told me."

"She told you what?"

"In India once, one night, she started to talk about herself. She usually never did, not seriously. She said her ex-husband caught her trying to seduce his brother. It didn't mean anything to me; I mean I didn't know who she meant. She must have known I would find out. It's true, isn't it?"

"So," Willi said. "What can I say? I found her trying to seduce him, yes, you could say that. I sent her away, and then her father sent her to Switzerland to work for his company. But there is something she did not tell you. Arul wouldn't have her. He told me what was going on. That's one reason she hated him."

"Did Arul have any faults at all?"

"You know he did."

"I don't remember what they were."

"Does it matter?"

"Yes. Now that I've lost Peter it matters very much. Linnet said you never gave her a divorce. Is that true?"

"Katrien, it was an arranged marriage for the benefit of our families. Divorce is not done. My father thought I was too harsh on her. My father thought it was Arul's fault. Arul joined his Christian group and left home in order to prove our father wrong. They didn't speak for three years. It was a very unhappy time. After Arul went to Switzerland Linnet returned to Delhi and pressed us for a formal divorce. My father refused to permit it, but then we discovered she had stolen much of Arul's money. She was very shrewd. My father cut her off, immediately. Suddenly divorce was permitted, but she disappeared. I was glad to forget her. I joined the international branch of the police. Occasionally I would hear rumors that she was involved in some scandal but I didn't pay attention. Then Arul came back with you and we stopped thinking about her. Until Banaras. Something you said in Banaras. Do you remember?"

"I told you she lived with us."

"You asked me if I knew her because she knew uncle Harish. You spoke of her as if you knew her well. In fact, she was following you until she could get Peter. Linnet killed Arul, you know, - and Jill Johnson - or, perhaps had them killed."

"*She* killed Arul? But why?"

"Arul had learned that Harish was an imposter - not our uncle, not even Indian. My mother had a brother who was presumed dead, twenty, maybe even thirty years ago. Harish was looking for an Indian "identity" to cover his other identities, since they had become legally troublesome to him. There were no financial benefits to becoming our "rediscovered" uncle, so it seemed safe. We all suspected him - everyone except mother. During his job as a night watchman, Arul uncovered this as well as some of Harish and Linnet's night work. He realized Linnet was deeply involved in the exploitation and sale of children. Arul cared, as you know, about social justice and he was going to go to the authorities. Linnet found out. It might have happened the same way if you told Arul of the threat on Peter. Remember - she knew Arul well."

"So why did she kill Jill? Did she want to sleep with her, too?"

"Do you want me to stop? We can talk about this later."

"No. Please. The American's thought I was involved in both murders. Now I think they were right. This morning - please talk to me, Willi. Anything to keep me from thinking about - I do want to know. I'm not wasting your time."

"You have never wasted my time," he said. "Jill was working for Stephen. She thought Stephen sent her to India to keep an eye on Linnet. We learned this in a statement yesterday. She decided to double-cross Linnet on her own, not trailing her quietly as Stephen wanted but blackmailing her - or trying to. I suspect Jill was causing Stephen trouble, so he decided to get rid of her by sending her to India, knowing Linnet would take care of her if she was a risk. The false link with PUCHSA was Jill's boyfriend's idea - one of Stephen's photographers who had a particular grudge against that organization. If Jill's link with child pornography was uncovered by the authorities - which seems likely - she would have been identified as part of PUCHSA; another religious organization involved in sexual scandal. It was clever. Unfortunately Jill was not clever. She bungled everything from the time she arrived in India. Linnet found herself being followed one night, and that was the end of Jill."

"How did you learn this?"

"We found letters from Linnet about Arul in Stephen's private papers. She was foolish enough to tell Stephen in writing that she had killed Arul, and why. I am surprised he kept the letter, even if it was in a special code they had. It is damaging evidence against him. The information about Jill came from this photographer's statement yesterday."

"Stephen liked to keep evidence. Did Linnet send your parents the photos of me?"

"How did you know about that?"

"The night they took the children away - after Arul died. I heard your mother say something to old Samuels about me and a photo. It was the tone of her voice. It didn't make sense unless she had seen one of Stephen's photos. Before that she was always very warm to me. Then suddenly she turned against me. I thought it was because she blamed me for his death. But it was the photos."

"She did blame you for his death, but it was because of the photo. They never thought you killed him. They thought you must have run with a bad crowd, and someone became jealous. I don't know what they thought. But they were very upset about the photo. As far as I know, there was only one. It came with a note that said something like, 'this is what your daughter-in-law is really like - is such a woman able to care for your grandchildren?' That's why they didn't permit you to get anything you might have had from Arul's death. I suspect Linnet thought that it would make it easier for her to get Peter in her power. She didn't count on my mother's strong hand." Willi decided not to tell her about the children in her chalet. Stephen would have known about the chalet, of course. This disposition of children was some part of his desperate moves at the end. There would be time for that later. "The photo of Peter was recent, done since you came to Geneva last year." he said.

"That's what Joanne said. And Arulai - have you heard what she told me?"

"No." he said. She told him. "And do you believe her?" Willi asked.

"You know, I do. Everything she said - well, it fit, somehow. It was those weeks - when I had the baby - " she hesitated - "it was the only opportunity they had to do anything like that. We were living with the Streckers. Jules was away. Joanne had to find a babysitter. She got one of the neighbors' daughters. I met her of course, after Christina and I came home. Elise - the babysitter - she was a little immature, but she was young. She seemed good with children - but that was before Arulai told me what happened. But why take the children for a ride and bring them home again, then kidnap Peter later? And why take photos at the farmhouse when they could have done it at the chalet?"

"I've talked to the Streckers," Willi said. "They didn't say anything about Arulai's story, but they did suspect he charmed one of the babysitters. Did the police question her?"

"Yes. She denied everything. I'm sorry, but I don't blame her. Why did you talk to the Streckers?"

Willi told her about the papers.

"And you're sure Peter's name wasn't there?"

"Yes. We found a false passport for Peter in Stephen's flat. Linnet wanted Peter all for herself, to raise as her own son. She had tickets to fly with him to England yesterday afternoon. They missed the flight. We think Stephen began to behave desperately once he realized the police had deciphered the papers. We probably will never know the whole story."

"I know." she said.

Willi finished the coffee in his cup. "Christina is the baby?" he asked.

Katrien nodded. "Arulai named her."

"She is sleeping?"

"No, she's downstairs with Mrs. Roberts - my landlady. She's a real character - like the box. She is always giving us medicine, food, chicken soup, anything to 'make it better'. She's very good with the children, but she talks - you have to laugh." Katrien stared across the room. "After the police left - I was afraid of what I might do, accidentally. Christina is so little. I thought of how I was when Arul died. I was afraid again - of myself. I told her I wanted to be alone to get the children's things together, so she took the baby. Do you understand?" She looked over at him, her eyes red, but dry.

"Yes." he said. There was a long silence between them. It stretched with the sun on the faded Turkish rug at their feet.

"I didn't hear until yesterday," he said after a long time. "Was it alright, having another child? I heard you were in hospital."

"That's where people often go to have babies. It was fine. Thank you for sending me out of India with my children."

"My father did that." There was a longer silence. "You don't have to talk about her."

"But you are giving me lots of opportunity," she looked at him, "In case I might?"

"Yes. Is it hard to talk about, because of Linnet?"

"Linnet didn't know about Christina," she answered. "I don't think she ever knew. It's surprising. I was sick in the morning in Banaras, but usually she wasn't home until noon. Ritu knew. She was scandalized," she smiled. "And you guessed."

"I was very impolite, I'm afraid," he said. "You scolded me about it. It was only a guess. It's good to see you will smile again."

"Not when I see Arulai. She's Peter's mother more than I am. It's so strange about death - that our lives go on at all. Arul's death changed my whole world, but I could still think about other things. Peter's death changes so little for me - perhaps I will be less afraid now, because I don't have to worry about Linnet and Stephen, or the photos. Peter's death is only part of that. This probably sounds cruel. But for Arulai, Peter's death will be everything."

"You will be there for her."

"Do you really believe I'm not a bad mother?"

"I do. We had a talk, you remember," he said, "In Delhi, last summer. After that, I thought differently about you."

"Hauz-Khas."

"Yes."

"Hauz-Khas was more than a talk." she said, looking at him strangely. "Hauz-Khas convinced you that I am a good mother?"

"You might say that. You were truly distressed about the children. I realized that night that you were not the sort who would work with Linnet, as I thought."

"You tested me?" she asked him, startled.

"Nothing so calculated," he said. "I heard how they treated you at my parent's house. I was very angry about it. I called Mrs. Mehta in Banaras to find out where you were staying in New Delhi. What happened after that - well, I certainly wouldn't call it a test," he smiled, "though parts of it, I admit, were a very pleasant surprise - "

"So - ," Katrien said quickly, "But when you visited us in Banaras, you made it seem as if we hadn't met since right after Arul died. I thought it was strange. Especially if you called Mrs. Mehta to find me. Why were you so secretive if she knew we had - talked in August?"

173

"I was in Banaras that week as a policeman, looking for Harish," he said. "I hoped for a more private visit, either with you or Mrs. Mehta, not a full, public family tea. I knew Linnet had some connection with Harish, and when you told me she was actually living with you, I was afraid he would hear that I was in the city. He did disappear again immediately after that. I think we have him now, with these papers. I didn't know how much I said in front of Ritu that day might - innocently - get back to Linnet, if she in fact lived with you. I also didn't know whether you wanted to be reminded of that day in New Delhi. You know, though" he paused, "I would like to see Christina now and then."

She looked at him in silence for a moment, then got up to look out the window again. "You're rather over-confident about her, aren't you?" There was an edge to her voice. "And about me? One single dark and rather consuming night and you assume you're the father of my child? I don't know how many people would be so sure of me."

"I am," he said. "I have a high opinion of you - even more in the last few days. I think there are several others who might argue that your reputation stands in my favor. Mrs Mehta, certainly. Joanne Strecker, probably. Maybe even this priest named Georges."

"You tease me - as usual. You haven't changed."

"Not at all." he said.

"Well, then," she shrugged, "You know you're right, as usual. I don't have to tell you anything." She looked over at him, amused. "You can see Christina whenever you like. You're Arulai's uncle, after all. I hope you don't think now you want to marry me."

"I haven't asked, have I?" he said, "Are you suggesting?"

"I'm not suggesting anything."

"Someone else has asked?" he said. She hesitated, confused. "Never mind," he went on. "Perhaps it is better that I don't know."

Katrien came over to the table and knelt down beside it, across from him, to gather up their coffee cups and spoons from the glass table top, putting them back into the wicker tray in the center of the table. For some time the only sound in the room was the clatter of pottery on glass. "It's not that," she said, finally. "I didn't want anyone in India to know about Christina because - in case I didn't ever get the children back. At least there would be one child no one could take away from me. You couldn't keep me from having it as long as you didn't know. But now - it has nothing to do with Linnet or anybody else. It's-" She looked at him but he said nothing.

"You're not like Arul," she continued, "but you do remind me of him. I didn't realize how much until I saw you in the street on Saturday night. I want to put all that behind me, Willi, to start over again, whatever that will mean. But - I hope - I hope we've known each other long enough that we don't need to avoid each other now just because of - Hauz-Khas."

"I hope not."

Just then someone knocked at the door. Willi stood up.

"You don't have to go," Katrien said.

"I think I will." he said. "You have other concerns right now. We can talk more later - if you want to."

"Yes," Katrien said. The knocking came again. She stood up from where she knelt by the table and went to the door. She opened it quickly before either of them could say anything else.

Arulai stood in the hall with Georges. She looked up at them, from Willi to Katrien.

"Georges met me after my swimming class and walked me home, Mama," she said. "But he wouldn't tell me anything. Is something wrong? Did they find Peter? Why are you here, Uncle Willi?" Georges and Willi nodded at one another silently. Katrien thought she glimpsed in Georges' face a warm and sudden light.

"Come in." She pulled the door wide. As they came in, Willi passed them silently and went out. He put his hand on Arulai's shoulder as they passed and then he went quickly down the steps. Katrien heard the outer door shut and his car engine start, then fade in the street. Slowly, she shut the door of the flat and turned toward the two who waited for her in the afternoon sun.

***

After Joanne Strecker came that afternoon to pick up Katrien and the children, the days that followed were very quiet ones for Georges. He missed hearing Arulai's voice singing to the radio as he went out into the hall each morning. He missed the sounds of footsteps across his ceiling in the evening. He still woke up in the middle of the night, but nothing woke him now except his own thoughts. There was no sound of a baby crying over his head. He felt lonely for the first time in many years.

On Tuesday, the day after Peter died, Katrien came to see him in the church office, to arrange a funeral service. Arulai did not come with her, but Willi did. Willi said very little during this meeting, but Georges could see that Katrien wanted him there. When Georges asked what was being done about the woman who died with Peter Willi answered, rather abruptly, that it had all been taken care of. Georges did not ask any more questions. On Thursday he performed the funeral service in the same small side chapel where Katrien and Arul were married. They buried Peter's small casket next to Katrien's mother, on a hillside just south of Lausanne. It was a very small funeral service, and afterwards they all fit into two cars and drove back to the Strecker's farm: Georges, Mrs. Roberts, the Streckers, Willi, Katrien, the children, and the Swiss policewoman who had followed the case from the day they brought in the photo. Joanne Strecker had a catered buffet waiting at the farm and they sat outside in the yard until dusk, eating, drinking and, now and then, talking.

Katrien talked very little, and mostly with Willi. When she and Willi went off for a long walk together, Georges sat in the yard in silence and found himself drinking rather a lot of wine. Across the yard, his mother was enjoying herself very much and not paying any attention to him at all. The policewoman came over and said he looked lonely. They talked about Peter for a little while. Then Arulai and Jules Strecker rescued him and took him on a walk through the farmyard, and then into the house to look at some of Jules' old books. By the time Mrs. Roberts was ready to go home, Georges felt just a little better. But then Joanne Strecker kissed him good-bye in a sad, comforting way, and looked at him as though she were sorry for him, and in a moment he felt miserable again. Katrien and Willi were coming in just then. Katrien told them that she and the children would be back at the flat the next day.

Georges drove his mother home very carefully that evening, and heard nothing at all that she said to him. Automatically, he kissed her goodnight and went up to his own flat and got undressed and went to bed without any conscious awareness of what he was doing. He did not sleep well. He got up several times in the night to pray for Peter Samuels, but all he could

177

think of was Katrien's face as she came in from her walk with Willi. He kept reminding himself of the best definition of love that he knew. It was by Democritus, in the fifth century BC. Right love, Democritus said, was longing without violence for the noble. Wasn't this what Georges wanted for Katrien? So why did it hurt so much?

Finally, at dawn, he gave up trying to sleep and went out for a walk by the lake. After the cafes opened, he sat at a table by the cafe where he took Katrien for lunch - was it only last Sunday? He ordered black coffee and drank it in silence, staring out at the water. After a long time, he remembered one of his parishioners in the hospital, an old lady, scheduled for surgery today. She would like a visit. It was not too early for that.

The weather was changing, but it was a hot day, and Georges kept himself very busy during most of it. When he got back to the church office, the phone kept ringing and, for once, he welcomed it. Someone let a beggar in and Georges found the man wandering through the sanctuary; he left after the secretary showed him the toilet and Georges gave him his own lunch. Several people came in for appointments and there was little time for Georges to think about himself again until late in the afternoon when he realized it was time to go home. The afternoon light was clear and sharp. Something about it reminded him of the way Joanne Strecker had kissed him goodbye after the funeral.

Georges got off the #2 bus and walked, very slowly, up the steep incline toward the rue de Nante. Katrien and the children would probably be back in the flat by now. His heart pounded in his chest. He really ought to get more exercise. He was all out of shape. Why was it so tiring, climbing the steep street,

178

today? He had done it all his life. He was just going home, after all. He stopped, halfway up, to wipe his forehead.

When he got to the house he found Arulai waiting for him. She sat out on the front steps, her hair in two braids over one shoulder. She was reading a book in the afternoon sun.

"There you are, Georges," she said, laying down the book. "I've been waiting and waiting for you."

"Now I know Arulai is back," he said. He pulled his handkerchief out of his pocket again and wiped his brow. "No one else reminds me how late I am."

"Georges!" Arulai said in a stage whisper. She leaned toward him, curling her finger, beckoning him to come closer. "I have a secret," she whispered. "But you can't tell Mama I told you. I think she doesn't want anybody else to know, yet."

Georges felt his pulse quicken. "Arulai," he said, "It's not always wise to tell other people's secrets." Besides, he thought to himself, there are some things I would rather not know.

"But I have to tell somebody," she said, "And I can't tell Peter anymore. Do you know what, Georges?"

Georges looked down at her, his vaguely troubled face reflected in her dark eyes, his heart still pounding in his ears. "What is it, Arulai?" he asked, after a long pause.

"My mother," she whispered. "I think she is going to marry my uncle Willi. I heard them talking about it. And after everything is settled with the police about the man who killed Peter, we might go back to India. Except they think it might not be safe, so we might stay here - I mean, in Switzerland. At least here, Mama said, people don't ask so many questions. I don't know why she said that. She's always telling me I ask too many." Her sandals scraped against the stones as she looked up at him, balding and sweating in his dark ordination suit.

"And are you happy about all of this?" Georges asked her gently in a very quiet voice.

"Well," she said, squinting and looking down at her shoes. "Mama is happy about it. And Uncle Willi - he's alright. And they promised me that no one will ever take me away from her like they took away Peter. And I never have to go back to live with my grandparents. Did you know I lived with them for a long time before we came here?"

"Yes," he said. "I remember you told me about it."

"But I'm sad, too, you know," she went on, squinting up into his face. "I'm sad because I miss Peter. And I'll miss you, Georges, if we go back to India."

"I would miss you too," he said. He looked down at the walk by her feet, at the Asterix book on the step. It was a book he had bought for her.

"Where are you going?" Arulai called as he picked up his briefcase. He turned away from her and began to walk out toward the street again.

"Just for a little walk," he answered.

"Wait! Can I come, too?" She hurried up from the step and ran after him. He stopped in the pebbled lane and turned back toward her.

"Of course, child." he said. "But first go tell your mother, so she doesn't worry."

About the author

S.R. Holman grew up in New England. She has lived
in Germany, Switzerland, and India.
A Harvard Divinity School graduate, she currently
does research in religion and public health.